The Idiot Box

by

Michael Elyanow

SAMUEL FRENCH

FOUNDED 1830

NEW YORK HOLLYWOOD LONDON TORONTO

SAMUELFRENCH.COM

**IMPORTANT BILLING AND CREDIT
REQUIREMENTS**

All producers of THE IDIOT BOX *must* give credit to the Author of the Play in all programs distributed in connection with performances of the Play, and in all instances in which the title of the Play appears for the purposes of advertising, publicizing or otherwise exploiting the Play and/ or a production. The name of the Author *must* appear on a separate line on which no other name appears, immediately following the title and *must* appear in size of type not less than fifty percent of the size of the title type.

Special thanks to Jeremy B. Cohen, David Elzer,
Mikhael Tara Garver, Sarah Gubbins,
Drew Larimore, JP Manoux, and Milo.

THE IDIOT BOX was produced by Open Fist Theatre Company (Amanda Leigh Weier and Martha Demson, producers) in Los Angeles in 2007. It was directed by Jeremy B. Cohen with sets by Donna Marquet; costumes by Alex Jaeger; sound by Lindsay Jones. The production stage management was Henry Lide with the following cast:

FIONA	Tisha Terrasini Banker
CONNOR	David Castellani
VERONICA	Corena Chase
OMAR	Joe Holt
CHLOE	Anna Khaja
RAYMOND	Conor Lane
BILLY	Dominic Spillane
HARVEY	Rod Sweitzer
MARK	Kelly Van Kirk
STEPHANIE	Amanda Leigh Weier

The World Premiere of THE IDIOT BOX was produced by Naked Eye Theatre Company, etc., etc. (Jeremy B. Cohen, Artistic Director; Geoffrey Barr, Managing Director) in Chicago in 2003. It was directed by Jeremy B. Cohen with sets by Brian Sidney Bembridge; costumes by Rachel Healy; sound by Andre Pluess; lighting by Jaymi Lee Smith. With the following cast:

FIONA	Kathy Logelin
CONNOR	Jim Slonina
VERONICA	Meghan McDonough
OMAR	Ansa Akyea
CHLOE	Beth Lacke
RAYMOND	Bradley Balof
BILLY	Brad Eric Johnson
HARVEY	Rom Barkhordar
MARK	Joe Dempsey
STEPHANIE	Lisa Rothschiller

CHARACTERS

(all early-to-mid-30's)

THE CAST REGULARS:

MARK, the Neurotic New Yorker. He's a paramedic.

CHLOE, the Spoiled Rich Girl. She's a curtain designer.

BILLY, the Sex-Crazed Dummy. He's a model.

FIONA, the New Age Hippie. She's an acupuncturist.

CONNOR, the Cynical Husband. He's an ad agency exec.

STEPHANIE, the Controlling Wife. She's a romance novelist.

THE GUEST SPOTS:

HARVEY. He's a doctor in the naval reserves.

RAYMOND. He's a drag queen/cabaret singer.

VERONICA. She's an Australian dog shusherer.

OMAR. He's a non-Caucasian PhD student.

THE PLACE

New York City.
Winter.

PRIMARY LOCATION

The living room of a split-level penthouse suite. The kitchen area and living room area are adjoining (think FRIENDS). There's a balcony upstage over-looking the city (FRASIER). A staircase leads to the top-floor bedrooms (EVERYBODY LOVES RAYMOND).

SECONDARY LOCATIONS

The Kaffeine Coffee Bar, a theatre, a subway car, Raymond's dressing room, Connor's room and Stephanie's office. These locations can be suggested through simple, specific objects and sounds: for example, the Coffee Bar might be represented by a bar table and stools, the subway car by subway seats and train wheels clacking. Scene changes should be lightning quick and energetic.

PRODUCTION NOTES

THE IDIOT BOX chronicles the deterioration of a TV sitcom as it descends into Reality. It takes familiar TV sitcom archetypes and conventions and then breaks the system down.

ACT ONE: at first, the sitcom should have the look and feel of a great, modern-day comedy. Peppy POP MUSIC should be used to link scenes. A LAUGH TRACK should be liberally employed. In terms of performance style, there might be a temptation to have the actors "act badly" like they do in "bad sitcoms." This is not the case. Before the point at which it all falls apart, the sitcom presented here should be an efficient, likeable, smart piece of popular entertainment at the top of its game. However...

...Once the sitcom starts breaking down, the look, feel and performance style should become much more natural. The laugh track should disappear altogether. ACT TWO should be played real and honest and gritty.

CANNED AUDIENCE RESPONSE KEY

☺ = full-on canned laughter
☺ = gentle canned laughter
☹ = fudd-up, creepy canned laughter/sound designer's choice
♥ = awww/sympathy sigh
☤ = silence

ACT ONE

[LIVING ROOM]. *A board game being played.* FIONA: *timing,* BILLY: *in hot seat,* CHLOE: *giving clues.* MARK *(in paramedic uniform) will soon enter from upstairs.*

FIONA. 20 seconds!

CHLOE. Boy, it's hot in here.

BILLY. Famous pick-up lines.

CHLOE. It's so hot my crust is turning brown.

BILLY. What a hooker might say. ☺

MARK. What're you guys doing?

FIONA. Playing a game.

CHLOE. Why don't you spread some butter on me?

BILLY. What a DIRTY hooker might say. ☺

MARK. *(entering)* The Pyramid? I love the Pyramid.

CHLOE. No, Billy, listen. Now that I've popped up and my crust is golden brown I'd go really good with some butter and jam right now because I'm a little slice of:

BILLY. Heaven.

FIONA. Time!

CHLOE. Toast. What A Slice Of Toast Might Say. Since when does a hooker ever say "My crust is turning brown?" Never. A hooker never says that. ☺

STEPHANIE *enters the front door, carrying a cardboard box with air holes.*

STEPHANIE. You guys are not gonna believe what I did! You know how Connor's been kinda depressed at his job lately?

FIONA. Ew, I hate Advertising. Thank God I got out of that.

9

MARK. Fiona, you're an acupuncturist. You never worked in Advertising.

FIONA. Sure I did. Don't you remember that whole thing where I got the promotion to Creative Director over that yucky old womanizer who didn't and then his hairdyer electrocuted him and suddenly he could read ladies' minds and he got me fired from the Nike account but then felt so bad about it that we had to make out?

MARK. That was Helen Hunt in WHAT WOMEN WANT.

FIONA. Yes, and I love that movie. ☺

STEPHANIE. Okay, back to me and the gift I just bought my sad husband.

The women crowd the box. ♥

STEPHANIE. It's a puppy! So he'll feel better. Isn't he the cutest?

FIONA. Cutest? This puppy is like sunshine in a box.

CHLOE. And he'll go with any color combination. Maltese?

STEPHANIE. Peekapoo!

MARK. Alright already. What about us?

BILLY. Yeah, I wanna peek at the peekapoo!

Now **BILLY** *and* **MARK** *reach down to pick up the pup. It BARKS and GROWLS like crazy.*

MARK. My God, that thing is vicious!

STEPHANIE. Hey! Bad boy! You are a very, very bad boy.

BILLY. Now *there's* something a hooker would say. ☺

BLACKOUT. We just witnessed a sitcom "teaser". Next, the THEME SONG plays and each of the six regulars are spotlighted in a fun and familiar montage. Then, LIGHTS UP on [**LIVING ROOM**]. **BILLY***'s reading a cereal box.* **MARK** *stands over him, drinking coffee.*

MARK. Can I read that when you're done?

*Billy **BILLY** hands the box over as a tired* **CHLOE** *enters from upstairs.*

CHLOE. Don't say it, I know. I look terrible. My clothes don't match, I have a hair bump and I think I just brushed my teeth with Neo-Sporin.

BILLY. Plus your shirt's on backwards.

CHLOE. *(realizing he's right)* Crudge!

MARK. What's wrong?

CHLOE. I'm exhausted, that's what's wrong! I couldn't sleep last night. Actually, for the past couple of weeks. I think something's on my mind. Just haven't figured out what it is yet.

MARK. Coffee?

> **MARK** *goes to get her some, but* **CHLOE** *thinks he's offering her his coffee and takes it.* ☺

CHLOE. Oh, what am I gonna do, Billy? I've got the biggest presentation of my life tomorrow – six clients from ABC carpets coming in to see *my* new curtain designs. I can't stumble in looking like Margot Kidder off her medication.

MARK. Or on.

CHLOE. I have to sleep tonight. I'm desperate.

BILLY. You wanna get some sleep, do what I do: Go see a play. ☺

CHLOE. Funny. ...You're serious.

BILLY. Think about it. You got your comfy seats, warm temperature, it's dark but not too. And nothin's more boring than theatre. All those "trained" actors talking in stuffy accents about "important things" that're supposed to make you "think", it's like having your own personal lullaby right in front of you.

CHLOE. Really?

BILLY. If there's one thing I learned from being a model, it's how to take care of yourself. We can catch a matinee right now. You'll sleep. I'll sleep. We'll wake up refreshed and camera-ready.

CHLOE. I dunno.

BILLY. I thought you were desperate.

CHLOE. I am desperate. *(looking at the open newspaper)* Okay, fine. Why don't we do... THREE SISTERS?

BILLY. Before or after the play? ☺

> **CHLOE** *exits as* **STEPHANIE** *and* **CONNOR** *enter.*

STEPHANIE. Aw, hun, wasn't this just the best morning?

CONNOR. It sure was – thanks to that 6AM walk with Sunshine.

MARK. You're in a good mood.

CONNOR. Why shouldn't I be? My brilliant romance novelist of a wife took a cue from the plot of the very first book she ever wrote and got her depressed husband a dog to cheer him up.

MARK. Speaking of books, Connor says the new one's almost done?

STEPHANIE. He-zell yeah. My writing hero, LaVyrle Spencer, author of THAT CAMDEN SUMMER, better watch her ass! I have been on fire with this love story! Phrases, paragraphs, metaphors: they've been coming out of me like... like... you know, some *thing* that comes out really, really fast. ☻

CONNOR. See? We're all in a good mood. Thanks to a little walk with Sunshine. Which we'll be doing again tonight at the park.

STEPHANIE. Pick you up at the cafe at 7. 7:15. Gotta stop off and get my ex-stepbrother a Bar Mitzvah present. Oh, and a kong. For Sunshine. Not my ex-stepbrother. Whatever. 7:15!

> *She blows* **CONNOR** *a kiss, exits. And a hurt* **CONNOR** *hops to couch.*

CONNOR. Ow, ow, ow... ☺

MARK. What's with the bunny-hop?

CONNOR. Sunshine.

BILLY. Your new puppy?

CONNOR. My new evil puppy. If I wasn't depressed before, I am now. Look what he did to my leg!

BILLY/MARK. Dude!

CONNOR. He's like a piranha with fleas. I'm telling you, Sunshine hates me.

MARK. Not just you. He went after me and Billy yesterday.

BILLY. Came this close to plucking the berries right off my branch. I need the berries! ☺

MARK. You gotta take that mutt back.

CONNOR. I can't. It makes Stephanie happy to see me happy even if I *am* miserable. Look, Sunshine probably just needs to get used to me. I'll take him for a walk on my lunch break and we'll sort this thing through.

MARK. Hey, on your walk – will you return this DVD for me?

CONNOR. Aw, man.

MARK. C'mon, it'll save me a trip. Besides, do you really want to say no to a paramedic, that brave public servant who –

ALL THREE. – saves lives sometimes at the risk of his own?

CONNOR. PATCH ADAMS?

MARK. What, I happened to be in the mood for a light dramedy about a med student who heals patients with laughter.

BILLY. You went to rent a porno and chickened out again, didn't ya? How many times I gotta tell you: just make a bee line for the backroom.

MARK. Hey, I'm making progress! At least I'm not stuck way back in New Releases anymore. I've moved up! I'm in Classic Drama now, baby!

CONNOR. So *that's* why we had to watch ZORBA THE GREEK! ☺

FIONA *and her boyfriend* **HARVEY** *– who's carrying a half-eaten breakfast tray – descend the stairs.*

CONNOR. Oh. Creepy boyfriend alert.

BILLY. Creepy? I think Harvey's cool.

CONNOR. Smart, nice *and* a doctor in the navy reserves? No. There's something about him I don't like.

MARK. You don't like anyone your sister dates.

CONNOR. I liked sweaty Lloyd from Montana.

MARK. Didn't he die of a heart attack three dates in?

CONNOR. And it was such a shame. ☺

> *HARVEY and FIONA arrive. HARVEY hands out three bags to:*

HARVEY. Connor. Billy. Mark. Thought of you while I was in Jakarta.

CONNOR. Gourmet fish crackers. Gee, thanks Harvey.

MARK. Well, I better get going. *(to CONNOR)* Don't forget to return the you-know-what.

HARVEY. I'm headed uptown if you gentlemen care to share a cab.

BILLY. Gentlemen? Yeah, sure.

> *HARVEY kisses FIONA; exits with BILLY and MARK.*

FIONA. Whoo! Is that tush not yummy on a stick? I'm telling you, Harvey could be the guy. *The* guy. You know what I got this morning? Breakfast in bed. We're talking pancakes, mochaccinos and a surprisingly poignant JUDGE JUDY.

CONNOR. That's nice. Out of curiosity: how's Harvey's heart? ☺

> *BLACKOUT. LIGHTS UP ON [A THEATRE].*
> *Sounds of a BAND PLAYING as Chekhov's THREE SISTERS is being performed offstage. BILLY's sleeping, but CHLOE... is riveted, moved. In a thick Russian accent:*

ACTRESS (OFF-STAGE). O, the band plays so bravely – you feel you want to live! Sweet Masha, dear Irina, don't you see? Time will pass, and we shall be forgotten, but our sufferings will turn to joy, kind sisters, for those who live after us. O, how the band plays! Another moment, and we shall know why we live and why we suffer... If only we could know. If Only We Could Know!

Audience APPLAUDS, "house" lights go up. **CHLOE** *wipes away her tears.* **BILLY** *wakes up, applauds along. Then he notices:*

BILLY. Oh my God.

CHLOE. I know. Look at me, I'm still shaking.

BILLY. You see her, too?

CHLOE. What?

BILLY. That superhot chick over there. She's totally checking me out. You're okay getting home without me, right? ☺

BILLY exits. An emotional CHLOE looks to the stage: it's a surprisingly non-sitcom moment. CHLOE exits. There's the sound of WIND blowing as OMAR runs in, just missing her. Another non-sitcom beat, and BLACKOUT. LIGHTS on [KAFFEINE COFFEE BAR] as we find STEPHANIE, at a bar table, reading LaVyrle Spencer's SEPARATE BEDS.

STEPHANIE. Oh, LaVyrle. How do you do it?

CONNOR enters, limping. STEPHANIE notices.

...What's with the limp?

CONNOR. Foot's asleep. What's with the telescope?

STEPHANIE. It's the present for my ex-stepbrother. Remember, he's having his Bar Mitzvah this weekend?

CONNOR. Oh, right.

STEPHANIE. I need you to box it up and send it out for me.

CONNOR. Sure.

STEPHANIE. And *not* pass it off onto someone else.

CONNOR. Like I ever do that.

STEPHANIE. Seriously? There's wrapping paper in the hutch. Don't use the one with the bunnies on it. Make sure you use scotch tape, not –

CONNOR. Masking. And use the good scissors.

STEPHANIE. Who knows me? Okay, we ready for that walk with Sunshine?

CONNOR. Yeah, about that. Listen, Steph, I –

STEPHANIE. What's wrong? Connor, do you not want to go to the park? *(gasps)* Do you not like Sunshine? ☺

CONNOR. No. No-ho-ho! I, I love Sunshine. I was... I just was hoping for a little you and me time. You know, one on one.

STEPHANIE. Ohhh, one on one. Maybe this will hold you over.

She kisses him. Audience goes "WHOOO!"

How was that?

CONNOR. Well... my participle's no longer dangling. ☹

STEPHANIE. OH MY GOD, what happened to your neck? *(spins him around)* There are scratches all over you! First you don't want to go to the park, now this. Connor, what is going on?

CONNOR. Okay, now, there's a really good explanation for this. And by good I mean bad because, well, um, you know that... new laundry detergent you got? I'm allergic to it!

STEPHANIE. Of course. And it's making you scratch, isn't it?

CONNOR. Like a dog! ☺

BLACKOUT. **[LIVING ROOM - NEXT DAY].**
FIONA, BILLY *and a yawning* **CHLOE** *play the Pyramid once again.*

FIONA. And... time!

BILLY. Countries in South America! Easy answer! Totally woulda gotten it if you had slept at the play like I said.

CHLOE. Billy, Anorexia and Bulimia aren't countries in South America.

BILLY. Then where are they? ☺

CHLOE *goes to get coffee just as* **CONNOR** *descends the stairs. His pants are torn.*

CONNOR. Okay, that is it! I am done playing with Sunshine. Why? I'll tell you why. Because he bit my ass, that's why!

FIONA. I guess you'll be wanting this then.

CONNOR. I don't think a business card's gonna stop the bleeding.

FIONA. No, see, one of my clients, I opened up her third chakra today – actually, I was totally going for the second when my hand slipped... this new oil I got is way too –

CONNOR. Good God, are we there yet?

FIONA. She's got a sister who can help you. Some world-famous dog trainer from Australia. Veronica something. She's in town taping a special for her show.

BILLY. Not Veronica Beecham?

FIONA. You know her?

BILLY. Everybody knows her. She's the Dog Shusherer. ☺

CONNOR. The what?

BILLY. The Dog Shusherer. She's like the Dog Whisperer, only quieter. This lady's amazing. She's like the whole reason people stopped saying "the dingo ate my baby."

House phone RINGS. **BILLY** *leaps to answer.*

BILLY. I got it I gotitIgotit! *(answering)* Yo! Heyyy, Ramona! I did? Oh. No, no, don't send it. I'm free now. Why don't you come straight over to my apartment after you get off work? Aw, come on. Come on, Ramona. Ramonaaa! ☺ Great. See you later. *(hangs up)* That was Ramona. I hooked up with her at the play last night. Left my wallet at her pad. She's bringing it by.

CONNOR/FIONA. Oh.

BILLY. Which is a total relief – not the wallet, the hooking up – cuz I been kinda off my game lately.

CONNOR/FIONA. Oh?

BILLY. Truth is, we never *really* hooked up, not in the umbilical sense. I mean, she brought me back to her place, but we never did it, not even close. She never even took her shoes off.

CONNOR/FIONA. Oh!

BILLY. But we did make out. For hours! Good kisser. Nice lip action, adventurous tongue style. Anyway, at some point she looks at her watch, gets all serious and goes, "You better leave." So I'm thinking either virgin or... well, virgin. ☺ Which is why I accidentally-on-purpose left my wallet behind so she'd have to see me again. Smart or what?

FIONA. Wait a minute. This woman: was she wearing a ring on her left hand?

BILLY. Yeah, why?

CONNOR. And did you notice any manly stuff laying around anywhere?

BILLY. Come to think of it, I did see a jockstrap in the bathroom. And I used a little of the Speed Stick that was hanging out by the sink.

CONNOR. Dude, she's married.

BILLY. Oh my God. You're right.

> **CONNOR** and **BILLY** *look to each other. A serious beat and then: they high-five!*

CONNOR/BILLY. Dude! ☺

BILLY. *(running upstairs)* I got myself a Married Girl! I better go find my Sexy Mix Tape!

FIONA. Alright, I'm outta here. Harvey's cooking me dinner and I don't wanna be late.

CONNOR. Dinner? Didn't he just take you out for lunch yesterday?

FIONA. You know what? I like Harvey. I like him a lot. And it wasn't lunch, it was high tea. We ate buttermilk scones and talked for three hours. I'm happy. It's time you stop digging around my dates for sniggly little nitpicky flaws.

CONNOR. What are you, Mother Goose?

FIONA. Okay, that's it. When it comes to Harvey, you're getting the mute button.

CONNOR. I'm your big brother! You can't mute me.

FIONA. What? Huh? Your lips are moving and all I hear is... bye!

CONNOR. Mute me all you want, he's still no dead sweaty Lloyd! ☺

> CONNOR *follows* FIONA *out. Finally, silence. A beat as* CHLOE *rests. Then, the sound of WIND... and a KNOCK at the door.*

OMAR (O.S.). Hello? Anybody home? Hello? Look, um. If you can, can hear me, I'm looking for a, uh, Chloe Schaeffer? Hello? Look, I just. I know how this is gonna sound – weird, um, odd – but I wrote her this letter. Nothing huge, just... thoughts. You know, thoughts. Anyway. Gonna slip it under the door. If you could, could just see that she gets it, I'd be... yeah.

> OMAR *exits.* CHLOE *picks up the envelope. Looks at it. BLACKOUT.* **[KAFFEINE - THAT NIGHT].** CONNOR *and* BILLY *with coffees as an excited* MARK *enters, hiding something behind his back.*

MARK. Gentlemen, you are looking at a changed man. Not only did I walk straight back to the Porno Section like I owned the joint... I bought, baby, I bought!

> *He pulls out a GARBAGE BAG full of DVDs.*

BILLY. Oh my God! It's like Christmas for perves. ☺

MARK. And you're not gonna believe who I bumped into. Harvey.

CONNOR. Harvey?

MARK. Harvey! He had an even bigger porno stash than me. And his selections? Let's just say they involved women of great size.

BILLY. Some men find large women very attractive.

MARK. Not large, Billy. Not zaftig. These women, they were all at least two hundred pounds overweight. You should have seen the titles: PLUMP FRICTION. SHE'S ALL FAT.

CONNOR. Oh my God.

MARK. YOU'VE GOT WHALE. ☺

CONNOR. Of course. It all makes sense now. The mochaccinos, the scones, the dinners... Fiona's dating a chubby chaser.

MARK. A what?

CONNOR. A chubby chaser. Men who only date overweight women.

BILLY. But Fiona's not –

CONNOR. Yet.

MARK. You don't think...?

CONNOR. Harvey's trying to fatten my sister up? Yes, yes I do.

MARK. Connor, this is serious. You better go tell her now.

CONNOR. I'm not telling her anything. She muted me.

BILLY. *(gets coat)* I know where Harvey lives. I'll go tell her.

MARK. Before you do, Ramona called.

BILLY. She did?

MARK. Twice. Said she really, really, really wants you to call her back.

CONNOR. You know what that means. She wants to tell you the truth and break it off. Your wallet's going back in the mail!

BILLY. No it's not. Because I am *not* calling her. Now Ramona will have to stop by here after work, at which point I'll go *to* work... my mojo that is. I ain't lettin this Married Girl go.

MARK. Wait a minute. Ramona's a Married Girl?

ALL THREE. *(serious beat, then high-fiving)* Dude! ☺

> **VERONICA BEECHAM** *(the Australian-accented Dog Shusherer) enters. Audience APPLAUDS the famous guest star.*

VERONICA. Oh, g'day. I'm looking for a Connor Dash. The doorman said I might find him here.

BILLY. It's Veronica Beecham!

MARK. You're even hotter in person did I just say that out loud?

CONNOR. I... I'm Connor Dash. I think.

VERONICA. Your sister told me about Sunshine. Case of the barkies, eh? Well, you're in luck. I've got a few hours before I'm needed back on the set, so let's take a geek at that pup of yours.

CONNOR. What about saving Fiona from the chubby chaser?

BILLY. Eh, she's a big girl. ☺

As they exit, BLACKOUT. **[LIVING ROOM].** **CHLOE**'s *sitting at the top of the stairs, holding* **OMAR**'s *unopened envelope. She tucks it away as* **VERONICA** – *carrying Sunshine in the box* – *enters with* **MARK** *and* **CONNOR.** *As* **VERONICA** *places the box downstage center:*

VERONICA. I think I have an idea of what's wrong with Sunshine. Just need to conduct a little experiment. You're all going to stack up shoulder to shoulder, facing Sunshine. You, too... Chloe is it? *(***CHLOE** *nods)* Okay, Connor, Mark. I want you both to march right up and pet the dog.

CONNOR *and* **MARK** *go to pet the dog. It BARKS wildly.*

CONNOR. You see? You see?!

MARK. I didn't even touch him!

VERONICA. Back to your original spots. Okay, eyebags, now you.

CHLOE *pets the dog. It makes calm, friendly WHIMPER-ING noises. Then, the DOOR OPENS and* **CONNOR** *over-reacts with:*

CONNOR. Don't freak out, Steph, I can explain – Fiona! What are you doing here?

FIONA. *(Entering.)* I just broke up with Harvey.

CONNOR. You did? Really? That must've been pretty awful.

FIONA. Actually, it was pretty easy. I just told him I was a country in South America. ☹

VERONICA. *(rising)* Ah, yes. Well, Connor, it *is* just as I thought. See, the problem with your dog is –

DOOR OPENS! It's an out of breath **BILLY**.

CONNOR. It's not what you think, Steph, I can – Billy! Way to go! Fiona totally freaked me out. You're supposed to warn me when Stephanie's coming.

BILLY *nods.* **CONNOR** *realizes.*

It's my wife. She can't see you. Hide!

VERONICA. Hide?

EVERYBODY. Hide! ☺

CONNOR *shoves* **VERONICA** *into the closet as everybody else assumes "casual" positions: laying on the couch, reading at the table. As this is happening,* **OMAR** *comes up to the door, sees* **CHLOE**. *She sees him. They stand still, connecting through the chaos. But then he exits, just as* **STEPHANIE** *enters.*

STEPHANIE. I called you at work today, why didn't you pick up?

CONNOR. Why? Why? WHY? Because... there was no work. It's... a holiday.

STEPHANIE. I'm not aware of any holiday.

CONNOR. No, not a holiday. But a holiday of sorts. It's... my birthday.

EVERYBODY. HAPPY BIRTHDAY! ☹

STEPHANIE. No, it's not.

CONNOR. No, it's not. Not here. Not in the real world. But at the agency it is. Eleven years ago today marks the first day I started working there. My work-birthday. Or as it's referred to in ad lingo: my wuhbuhday.

EVERYBODY. HAPPY WUHBUHDAY! ☺

STEPHANIE. I'm taking a bath. Whatever you've done with

my husband, make sure he's returned when I get out.

She goes to hang up her coat in the closet.

CONNOR. Here, let me get that for you.

STEPHANIE. I got it.

CONNOR. I never get to hang up your coat. Come on, I insist.

STEPHANIE. Since when are you an insister?

CONNOR. Since my wuhbuhday. ☺

STEPHANIE. Connor, stop. You know there's a certain way I like to hang my coat, besides there's stuff in the pockets and –

She opens the closet door, finds **VERONICA** *holding a telescope. Audience GASPS.*

STEPHANIE. Aha! I knew it! You *have* been been having an affair!

CONNOR. What?

STEPHANIE. The scratches down your back? The weird behavior? The woman I'm standing across from who's hiding in our closet? If she's not your mistress, then who is she –

VERONICA. Veronica Beecham.

STEPHANIE. – and why is she holding my ex-stepbrother's Bar Mitzvah present? You were supposed to box that telescope up and send it out. What happened?

MARK. Uh, Connor... that box was yours?

CONNOR. Yeah, why?

MARK. I kinda used it to stash my porno.

CHLOE. Oh my God. Connor, remember when you asked me to wrap up the box at the foot of the stairs and send it out?

CONNOR. Oh my God.

MARK. Oh *my* God! My porno! It's the Bar Mitzvah present!

FIONA. Where are you going?

MARK. Where else? Temple Beth El!

EVERYBODY BUT STEPHANIE. I'll go with! ☺

STEPHANIE. Everybody stay! *(to* **CONNOR***)* I can't believe you. Passing the buck, hiding a mistress, making me drop my coat!

CONNOR. Steph, please. You don't understand. She's not a mistress, okay? She's... the Dog Shusherer. Her name's Veronica Beecham and she fixes bad dogs.

VERONICA. Your husband's telling the truth.

MARK. Seriously. Sunshine's been biting Connor ever since you got him. Right, Chloe?

CHLOE. Huh? Oh, yeah. That's why he asked me to send out the gift.

FIONA. If you're gonna blame anybody, blame me. I told Connor to call Veronica.

STEPHANIE. So those scratches... they're because of Sunshine?

CONNOR. I'm sorry.

STEPHANIE. Why didn't you tell me?

CONNOR. I don't know. I thought I could fix him before you found out. You did something so nice for me and I didn't want you to be disappointed, so I lied.

STEPHANIE. Oh, Con. I've been lying, too. My writing hasn't been going as well as I'd like. I'm nowhere near done with my romance novel. Bet my hero LaVyrle Spencer, author of A HEART SPEAKS, never has writer's block. Anyway: I'm sorry.

CONNOR. Best Wife Ever.

STEPHANIE. Best Husband Ever.

They hug. ♥

But the next time I get you a dog and he starts attacking you, just tell me.

VERONICA. Oh, it's doubtful you'll run into that problem again.

CONNOR. What do you mean?

VERONICA. I'm afraid Sunshine is a masculinus odiumnus. A man-hater. That's why he tried to disembowel the blokes but he's a lamb with the sheilas. It happens. Some male dogs just turn on their own gender. I think it'd be best if I found Sunshine a new home. I know of a lesbian commune in Sydney that'd love to have him. You understand.

They all nod. And just as **VERONICA** *walks off with the box of Sunshine,* **RAMONA** – *clearly a man in drag – enters.*

RAMONA. Oh. Hello. I'm here to see –

BILLY. Hey, Ramona! It's Ramona everybody!

RAMONA. Oh, what a cute dog.

As she leans over to see it, Sunshine BARKS more fiercely than ever! And **CONNOR** *leans over to* **BILLY** *with:*

CONNOR. Looks like your Married Girl is a Single Guy. ☺☹

BLACKOUT. This marks the end of an episode. But as OUTRO music plays and everyone exits, a confused **CHLOE** *stays put. THEME MUSIC comes up again, but distorted now. Static CRACKLES. Lights FLICKER.* ☹

CHLOE. Wait. What's happening? Where's everybody going? Hey! Stephanie? Come back. Fiona! I'm talking. Can't you hear me? *(looks up)* Oh God. Oh God, no!

The fun house is a madhouse now. Then: MUSIC cuts short, LIGHTS go UP. Silence. A DOORKNOCK. A beat (and it's real). A KNOCK again. **CHLOE** *goes to the door, but doesn't open it.*

CHLOE. ...Who is it?

OMAR (O.S.). Hello?

CHLOE. Who is it?

OMAR (O.S.). Oh, uh. Hi. You don't know me, but.

CHLOE. Yes?

OMAR (O.S.). I'm ...looking for Chloe Schaeffer.

CHLOE. Are you that...?

OMAR (O.S.). Yes.

CHLOE. From before?

OMAR (O.S.). Yes.

CHLOE. I'm sorry. Do I know you?

OMAR (O.S.). No, like I said.

CHLOE. How did you get up here?

OMAR (O.S.). Oh. Your doorman. I hope it's okay. I'm not going to hurt you.

CHLOE. Hurt me?

OMAR (O.S.). If that's what you're worried about.

CHLOE. I wasn't.

OMAR (O.S.). Good, because I'm not. I'm very, you know... I have a cat. My point being I know this seems a little strange, but.

CHLOE. Look, I really should.

OMAR (O.S.). If you give me a minute to explain. Just a minute. Please.

A beat, and **CHLOE** *opens the door.* **OMAR** *stands before her. The two are rapt. Then:*

CHLOE. You were going to –

OMAR. Right.

CHLOE. – explain.

OMAR. Right. Um. Last week. I saw you at the theatre. THREE SISTERS? I'm afraid I was watching you throughout most of the performance.

CHLOE. Oh.

OMAR. So I came to –

CHLOE. Right, no.

OMAR. – say I'm sorry.

CHLOE. I see.

OMAR. Did you get my letter?

CHLOE. Yes.

OMAR. You did?

CHLOE. Yes.

OMAR. Because in it.

CHLOE. I didn't open it.

OMAR. No?

CHLOE. I don't know you. No offense.

OMAR. Right.

CHLOE. I'll open letters from people I know, acquaintances, fabric representatives even, but strangers –

OMAR. No, right. Well. It just said I'm not stalking you. In the letter. Among other things. Thoughts. But emphasizing that I'm not a stalker. I mean, I did follow you home and it took me a while to get your name from the doorman. But that's it.

CHLOE. Ah. Relief.

OMAR. Believe me, I never do this sort of thing. Ever. But... here I am.

CHLOE. There you are.

OMAR. ...I'm sorry. I'm gonna. Sorry.

He exits. But just as **CHLOE** *is about to close the door:*

No, wait. Please. The thing is. I was watching the play and somewhere toward the end of the first act I happened to take my eyes off the stage for a second and... I saw you sitting across from me and you were so completely "in it", I mean, leaning forward, tears in your eyes, you know, and I was thinking, Yes! That's the power of Chekhov. How he manages to just nail it. All the hope and dread and joy and secrets we keep locked up inside our hearts and our heads and never say out loud and Moscow, oh, Moscow. Which all sounds like a line, a very bad line, but it's not and I know I don't know you, it's just that you left the theatre so quickly and I wanted to tell you that I felt the same way, too. ...I would really like to spend even just an hour getting to know you. You must be the most extraordinary person. And I must be a complete idiot for talking all this time and not introducing myself. Omar Jackson. Blabbermouth.

CHLOE. Chloe Schaeffer. Insomniac.

Then, in the distance, a SOUND CUE that is **CHLOE***'s warning: peppy BRIDGE MUSIC approaching.*

You wanna go for a walk? Quick.

They exit. BLACKOUT. BRIDGE MUSIC louder as LIGHTS UP on **FIONA** *and* **STEPHANIE** *at the couch:* **STEPHANIE** *on her laptop,* **FIONA** *reading a novel.* **CONNOR** *bounds downstairs just as the MUSIC turns to crackling STATIC, then SHORTS OUT.* ☠ *The machine has broken. But our friends don't know it. Yet. For now, there's just... this feeling.*

CONNOR. ...Wifey, Sistery. Whatcha reading there?

FIONA. Steinbeck. THE GRAPES OF WRATH.

CONNOR. Funny. ...You're serious.

FIONA. Don't you remember how obsessed I was with this book in high school? Remember I dressed up in farmer clothes for like two months? Took all your flannel shirts?

CONNOR. THE GRAPES OF WRATH? Really?

FIONA. You'd like it. There's a brilliant scene at the end where this woman breast feeds an elderly man who's starving to death. It's all very Tragedy meets Sensuality.

CONNOR. Boobies? Cool. ☠ *Boobies. Cool.*

Still ☠*. Odd. Then:* **MARK** *and* **BILLY** *rush down the stairs. Also, they're both in bad fake police officer costumes.*

MARK. Bye!

BILLY. See ya!

CONNOR. Whoa, hold on... Police caps, billy clubs, shiny badges. Is there a Village People concert I don't know about? ☠

MARK. You are not gonna believe this.

BILLY. We were in the car and got pulled over for speeding.

FIONA. That *is* unbelievable! ☠

MARK. He's not done.

FIONA. There's more?!

BILLY. We got pulled over by these two gorgeous – I mean GEE-orgeous ladycops. They're this close to giving us a ticket, but Mark talks them out of it by saying, get this, we're *also* cops.

MARK. Cops from Loozeeanna. On vacation in the big city. Away from our wives, our kids.

BILLY. No responsibilities, no ties.

MARK. Now we're meeting them for drinks in what could possibly be the best scheme ever!

STEPHANIE. Wait a minute. You guys pretended to be married cops to get out of this ticket and now you're going on a double date?

CONNOR. Aw, Steph, let them have their fun.

STEPHANIE. Fun?

CONNOR. Uh-oh.

STEPHANIE. Deceiving women in hopes of scoring? Pretending you've got a wife at home that you look forward to cheating on? That's what you consider fun? That's how little you regard marriage?

CONNOR. Jeez, what's with you?

STEPHANIE. Me? Why is it always "what's with me?" What's with you? Just because I've been trying to write this stupid romance novel for a whole year and –

STEPHANIE.	**CONNOR.**
– and the only thing that has come out of me is a desire to eat more and more Pringles making me fatter and sadder and more blocked by the day no matter how many times I try to channel my hero LaVyrle Spencer doesn't mean anything is *with* me and you smothering me like some fucking retarded two-year-old doesn't help!	I know, hun. You're beautiful. It's okay.

CONNOR. ...What did you just say?

STEPHANIE. I, I don't know.

MARK. *(lightening the mood)* Okay! We better hit the subway if we want to make that movie.

CONNOR. What movie?

MARK. You know, the movie that will cheer your wife up and not make us all so terrified she's going to skin us alive.

STEPHANIE/CONNOR. Ohhh, that movie.

> *BLACKOUT. A spotlight shines on* **RAMONA** *(the drag queen). She's in full cabaret regalia, singing a song in the style of Carey & Fischer's "You've Changed".*

RAMONA.

EVERYTHING'S DIFFERENT NOW
I CAN FEEL IT IN THE AIR AND HOW...
COULD YOU DO WHAT YOU DID
AND SAY WHAT YOU SAID
AFTER ALL OF THE TIMES
YOU'D GIVEN ME... YOUR FRIENDSHIP
YES, EVERYTHING'S DIFFERENT NOW

> *LIGHTS UP on the gang in* **[A SUBWAY CAR]**. **RAMONA** *sings to them. They can't see her. Like a fairy godmother,* **RAMONA** *crosses over to them, singing in their ears...*

RAMONA.

DON'T YOU REMEMBER WHEN
WE SWORE OUR AIN TRUE LOVE AND THEN
O, HOW THE BIRDS DID SING
BUT YOU HAD TO GO AND BLOW EVERYTHING
NOW EVERYTHING
IS DIFFERENT NOW

> **RAMONA** *exits.*

MARK. Did you guys hear that?

BILLY. Hear what?

MARK. Nothing.

FIONA. Hm.

MARK. What?

FIONA. Nothing. ...Maybe it was –

MARK. Yes!

FIONA. – nothing.

CONNOR. No! It was something.

STEPHANIE. What was something?

CONNOR. That nothing.

BILLY. That nothing was something?

MARK. Something is off.

STEPHANIE. Me.

BILLY. What?

STEPHANIE. I'm off. To the office.

CONNOR. You're leaving?

STEPHANIE. Right.

CONNOR. Me?

STEPHANIE. Write.

CONNOR. You are?

STEPHANIE. Write. I can't write.

FIONA. She's blocked.

BILLY. She's off.

> **STEPHANIE** *has exited.*

MARK. Something is wrong.

CONNOR. My wallet's gone.

MARK. See?

BILLY. You better report it.

MARK. I'm an officer.

FIONA. Funny.

MARK.	**CONNER.**
Maybe you should. I was gonna say. You go. No, you. You. Stop it!	Maybe you should. I was gonna say. You go. No, you. You. Stop it!

MARK. You stop it!

CONNOR. You stop... okay.

MARK. I was gonna say, just borrow some money.

CONNOR. No, I think I'm just gonna get off here. I, I can't breathe.

MARK. We'll come with. It's our stop anyway.

Everyone but **FIONA** *exits. She stays behind, sighs. Relief? A beat, and* **HARVEY** *enters.*

HARVEY. *(surprised)* Fiona?

FIONA. Harvey?

BLACKOUT. **[LIVING ROOM].** **CHLOE** *and* **OMAR** *enter from their cold walk outside.*

CHLOE. A walk in the dead of winter, whose dumb idea was that? I'll take your – thank you.

As she hangs the coats up and, ever the good host, makes Cheez Whiz 'n crackers:

OMAR. I can't believe all six of you live here.

CHLOE. Yep. Six friends, eight rooms, one big penthouse in the Big Apple.

OMAR. This really is amazing. How did you find this place?

CHLOE. Oh. Well, Mark's grandmother gave it to him but only on the condition that Mark would be married by his 25th birthday so Mark (who had no serious girl-friend at the time but wanted the penthouse really bad) asked his best friend Connor to ask his sister Fiona if she'd pretend to be his wife – Mark's, not Connor's, because that would be incest and ewww – so Fiona said yes but only on the condition that Mark would give not only her but Connor and his wife, Stephanie, a place to stay rent free because, as luck would have it, this was right when Connor and Stephanie's apartment had burnt down in a freak grease fire and Fiona's whole building suddenly went condo, but the day of the wed-ding Fiona got cold feet and couldn't go through with it even though it was a fake wedding so Mark grabbed his high school yearbook, closed his eyes, pointed to a page and picked guess who, me, called me up, asked if we could make this arrangement and I said yes right away because oddly enough this was the very same day that I quit the family business – rubbers, don't ask – and my father threw me out and I had nowhere to go so I took off right away but by a strange twist of fate there was traffic and I ended up being late for the ceremony and that's when Mark's grandma Shirley showed up so Mark had no choice but to introduce Connor's wife Stephanie as his bride-to-be and of course that's when Fiona – who didn't know about Stephanie's involvement – stepped forward and introduced herself as Mark's bride-to-be, which was followed a second later by me introducing myself as – yep – Mark's bride-to-be, which of course made Mark look the world's biggest bigamist, and that's when Billy – who was at the time just one of the caterers coincidentally passing by – pretended to be Fiona's husband, saying that she was drunk and possibly bipolar and Connor did the same with Stephanie just so the whole cover wouldn't be blown which thankfully it wasn't because it's what got us all started living together as one big family.

OMAR. Wow. That's really fortunate how everything resolved itself in the end.

CHLOE. I never thought of it like that but, yeah, I guess it is.

OMAR. So Mark's grandmother still thinks you two are married?

CHLOE. Who? Oh, yeah. She doesn't come around that much, though. Just in like November and May. Sometimes February. You want something to drink? Beer? Wine? We've got a bottle of scotch here somewhere.

OMAR. I'm good.

CHLOE. Or, you know, if you're not a drinker we've got milk. Ah, yes, here we are. A very nice two-percenter. *(smells the milk; it's bad)* Apparently vintage.

OMAR. Really, I'm fine.

CHLOE. So... nothing?

OMAR. *(sensing her discomfort)* Maybe some, yeah, I'll take some water. Where are the glasses? I'll –

CHLOE. That's okay. I got it.

  . *BLACKOUT.* **[SUBWAY CAR].** **FIONA** *with* **HARVEY**.

HARVEY. So can I ask you something?

FIONA. Actually, no. I'm just gonna pretend you're not here and sing a royalty-free song from the public domain: *I ain't got nobody* –

HARVEY. How come you don't return my calls?

FIONA. *Nobody cares for me, nobody* –

HARVEY. And why'd you break up with me like that? Huh? A person doesn't do that, a *person* doesn't tell her boyfriend at a romantic dinner that she's bulimic as a means to break up. And, and mind you, it's not even true. You're neither bulimic nor anorexic. But I let you go anyway, because you were so freaked out by my fetish and all.

FIONA. Is that what that is, a fetish?

HARVEY. Yeah. I like fat women.

FIONA. No, you like skinny women who you can make fat.

HARVEY. It's called Feeding.

FIONA. What?

HARVEY. It's called Feeding. Technically, I'm a Feeder. The term has its roots in agriculture – livestock, what have you – but in a Feeder's case it applies to girlfriends.

FIONA. Okay, gross.

HARVEY. Hey, I only do it if they're into it. Most are. Last girl I dated gained like eighty pounds. It was awesome.

FIONA. Well I'm not into it. Hence, the bulimia.

HARVEY. Okay, point well taken. Not for you. I was wrong, I should have been more up front about my motives and for that I apologize. Truth is, I thought you were enjoying yourself. You never complained.

FIONA. Had I known what you were doing, I would have. It's disgusting.

HARVEY. What's disgusting? Two consenting adults explor-
ing the body? I guarantee you there's nothing more
intimate. My second wife, right? When we first started
doing it – late at night in bed, we'd just lay around and
listen to the pores of her skin expanding. It was beautiful. This breathy little squeak became a metaphor: as
my wife grew, so did our love.

FIONA. Oh my God. What is wrong with you?

HARVEY. Don't do that, don't turn this on me.

FIONA. I'll do whatever I (want) –

HARVEY. There's more to you, Fiona. I know there is. And
I'm not talking just sexually. Deep down... you are a
complex character.

A beat. She's caught.

FIONA.	**HARVEY.**
Hummala bebhuhla zeebuhla boobuhla hummala bebhuhla...	Wow. That is so fucking pathetic. Just when I thought I couldn't feel any sorrier for you.

FIONA. You feel sorry for me?

HARVEY. Yeah. You act like a child. And when you don't act
like a child, you act like an idiot.

FIONA.	**HARVEY.**
Are you – whuh – are you kidding me? You try to fatten me up and when you can't get your sicko fetish way you try to pressure me into –	You're in your thirties for godsakes! Aren't you exhausted, all this I'm gonna stand over here and sing crap?

HARVEY. I'm not talking just sex! Sex is just one compo-
nent. One thing you choose to keep hidden. I am talking
about you. *All* of you. The whole Fiona. I see what you hide
in your bag. The books you read.

FIONA. Everybody reads Steinbeck.

HARVEY. No. Not everybody reads Steinbeck, Fiona. Not

everybody reads The Economist – cover to cover – every week.

FIONA. Okay.

HARVEY. Not everybody drives five hours to hear Noam Chomsky lecture on –

FIONA. Okay.

HARVEY. – market democracy or registers with the ACLU or goes to –

FIONA. All right! Jesus!

HARVEY. – goes to exhaustive measures to pretend she's some flighty, wind-in-her-hair hippie just to cover up the fact that she's really, what, a scared little girl who's afraid her friends won't like her when they discover there's actual sophistication rattling around in that ditzy little skull (of hers).

FIONA. Okay. Stop. I'm gonna stop you right there. You know, just because we went out a few times, don't presume you know me and don't presume I don't know what I'm doing. How much money you think you spent on me when we were dating? Five hundred? Eight hundred? No. It was more. Much. Men buy me dinners, Harvey. Men buy me drinks. I get into the best clubs. Best concerts. Premieres, fashion shows. I've dated A LOT of hot boys and for the past eight years, I've had free rent in a Manhattan penthouse. I haven't had to pay for anything – quite literally – since I was TWELVE. That's what being a so-called flighty, wind-in-her-hair-hippie has gotten me.

HARVEY. Good for you. Looks like it's come with no price at all.

FIONA. Sarcasm? Really?

HARVEY. You're a fraud.

FIONA. Why? Because I choose to keep some things private?

HARVEY. Because nobody, not even your closest friends, know *you*.

FIONA. Nobody needs to know me. I'll let people in when I want to let people in.

HARVEY. And when will that be? When will you finally decide to let us in?

FIONA. Oh, Harvey. FUCK OFF.

A beat, and then just before she exits the subway car:

FIONA. You coming?

> *BLACKOUT.* **[LIVING ROOM].** CHLOE *and* OMAR
> *on the couch.*

CHLOE. I guess I've always liked it. It's fun, lifting them up, separating them. The biggest challenge, of course, is to keep them from sagging. And I always go with gold tassels because it makes people want to touch 'em all the more. Anyway. That's how I got into the curtain making business. What about you?

OMAR. Just finished my dissertation.

CHLOE. Oh, a professor.

OMAR. Not yet. One day.

CHLOE. What's it on?

OMAR. Media stuff. It's really boring.

CHLOE. I like being bored. I've seen COLD MOUNTAIN six times.

OMAR. Trust me, it's a date killer.

CHLOE. Is that what this is? A date?

OMAR. Informally.

CHLOE. So let's make it formal.

OMAR. All right. Would you like to go out?

CHLOE. Lemme think about it.

> *As* **CHLOE** *thinks,* **MARK** *(unseen by them) heads down from upstairs. His hair's messed, cop uniform's unbuttoned. He stops when he sees* **CHLOE** *with* **OMAR.** *Observes instead.*

OMAR. Come on, dinner and a play. It's nothing.

CHLOE. Yeah, sure, what the heck.

OMAR. Great. This will be our post-date nightcap. I've already picked you up and taken you out to eat.

CHLOE. Pizza?

OMAR. Seafood.

CHLOE. Smart.

OMAR. I did my homework.

CHLOE. And a great choice of theatre.

OMAR. Again, homework.

CHLOE. Everything was just wonderful. I felt lousy for ditching you.

OMAR. Hm?

CHLOE. At intermission. I really needed to pee.

OMAR. That's okay. It gave me time alone to work through self-esteem issues.

CHLOE. Hey, that's what I was doing. Well, that and the peeing.

OMAR. A multi-tasker.

CHLOE. I was stressed.

OMAR. First dates are hard.

CHLOE. Impossible.

OMAR. All those awkward pauses...

CHLOE. Second guessing...

OMAR. Not to mention the attempts to impress.

CHLOE. I'm still kicking myself for saying "The mahi-mahi was yummy-yummy."

OMAR. And then there's the kiss.

CHLOE. I was nervous.

OMAR. So was I.

CHLOE. I'm glad we got it out of the way early.

> **OMAR** *kisses* **CHLOE.** *It's magical. Then:*

OMAR. Functionality and Representation of Ethnicity in 21st Century American Storytelling.

CHLOE. Hm?

OMAR. My disserta –

CHLOE. – tation, right. Right.

OMAR. It's a critique on how, in modern media, Blacks, Latinos, Asians, Middle-Easterners and so on, continue to be used as mere plot devices, existing only to give the white leads permission to change – usually by inciting them to act upon their sexuality or fear or anger or whatnot. Just once, I'd like to see a story where a non-white person comes in and he – or she – doesn't end up changing the lives of the white people he (or she) surrounds. *(then:)* What?

CHLOE. Nothing.

OMAR. It's boring, isn't it? Pretentious.

CHLOE. Not at all.

OMAR. What?

CHLOE. I like you. You're not funny.

> *BLACKOUT.* **[KAFFEINE].** **CONNOR** *sits, waiting. Nervous.* **VERONICA** *enters.*

CONNOR. Thanks for coming on such short notice.

VERONICA. No worries. Don't need to be on the set till half-past.

CONNOR. Mate. ☠

VERONICA. Huh?

CONNOR. Mate. You know, everybody says "mate" in Australia. "No worries, mate." "Hand me the crate, mate." ☠

VERONICA. You mentioned an emergency.

CONNOR. Yes. My wallet was stolen today.

VERONICA. Aw, that's a shit house.

CONNOR. And as I was walking back from the police station, I. I couldn't stop thinking. About Sunshine. I mean, this dog. He hates men, right? But he's a *man* himself. A male of the species. I think – and I'm no Dog Shusherer – but I think the reason Sunshine hates men is because he hates what is male about himself.

VERONICA. That's the emergency? You needed to pose a theory?

CONNOR. No. No! Well, yes, but it's no theory. It's true. Because if anyone knows where he's coming from, it's me. Which makes me the only one.

VERONICA. The only one what?

CONNOR. The only one can save him. Veronica, I can save Sunshine.

VERONICA. Okay, Connor, let's not – I mean, look. Even if you're right, even if Sunshine does hate what is male about himself, it doesn't matter. Next week he'll be Down Under at a lesbian commune, never to be around another man again.

CONNOR. Right, but see: why? Why isn't it a good thing to be around men? You're around them all the time, aren't you, on the set? Isn't it a good thing?

VERONICA. Connor, this (isn't) –

CONNOR. When did it stop being good? To be around men? To be a man? And why am I so depressed? I wake up in the morning and my head is so heavy I can barely lift it off the pillow. But I slap on a smile and I go to work and I pay my bills. Every day. And I come home. Every day. To a wife. Who is controlling and hostile. To me. But I make love to her anyway. Because this is what a man is supposed to do. So I do it. I do all these things – smile, work, bills, love – every day of my goddamn life, and still, *still* I get pick-pocketed.

VERONICA. Connor...

CONNOR. So this dog. This dog. If I can just get him to, if I can get him to stop barking at men, at his own man-ness... maybe I can find a way to do the same for myself.

He hands **VERONICA** *an envelope.*

Stephanie doesn't know about it, but I've been keeping this money aside, in a separate bank account, you know, just in case. You know. Anyway. I called your agent.

VERONICA. *(pulls out a check)* You giving me the razz?

CONNOR. I think I worked out a fairly lucrative deal. For you.

VERONICA. *(looks at the check)* Gads. Connor.

CONNOR. There's more to come. I'm cashing in my 401K. I don't care, I don't need a future. I need a... a *now*. Just please. I'm begging. Help me.

VERONICA. Help you what?

CONNOR. Teach me to be a Shusherer.

> *BLACKOUT.* [**LIVING ROOM**]. **OMAR** *with* **CHLOE** *on the couch.* **MARK** *still watching, but will soon head back upstairs.*

OMAR. I should get going. It's late.

CHLOE. It is.

OMAR. I've got a class to teach in eight hours.

CHLOE. I've got work in seven.

OMAR. I should get going.

> *But he doesn't. And* **CHLOE** *doesn't push him. LIGHTS DIM as a SPOT SHINES on* **RAMONA**, *once again singing, some time during which she'll walk into the living room set and sing to* **CHLOE**. *They will exchange a deep, connective glance.*

RAMONA.

DON'T YOU REMEMBER WHEN
WE SWORE OUR AIN TRUE LOVE AND THEN
O, HOW THE BIRDS DID SING
BUT LOOK AT HOW YOU
HAVE CHANGED EVERYTHING
YES, EVERYTHING
YOU'RE DIFFERENT NOW

> *BLACKOUT. Lights on* [**RAMONA's DRESSING ROOM**] *as* **RAMONA** *takes off her wig, jewelry, make-up. Underneath is a handsome man with a great sense of humor.* **HIS** *name is* **RAYMOND**. **BILLY** *enters in his cop duds.*

BILLY. What did you do to me?

RAMONA/RAYMOND. Billy?

BILLY. In my jacuzzi, right now –

RAYMOND. Who let you back here?

BILLY. In my jacuzzi, I got two hot ladycops looking for a little enforcement if you catch my drift and I couldn't... I can't... What did you do to me?

RAYMOND. You need to keep your voice down.

BILLY. Did you turn me fag?

RAYMOND. And now you need to leave.

BILLY. Why?

RAYMOND. Because you don't know what you're saying and you're being an asshole.

BILLY. You tricked me.

RAYMOND. Uh, I didn't do anything but go see a matinee.

BILLY. You were dressed like a girl.

RAYMOND. I was going to work after and I knew I wouldn't have time to change.

BILLY. What about that night you came to my apartment?

RAYMOND. *(laughs, then:)* Oh, you mean that night where you thought you could screw with me? That night where I left you messages saying it was imperative for you to call me back and you didn't? Because if it's *that* night, then hell yeah I came over dressed like a woman cuz I thought, fuckit, if he's gonna play games, so am I.

BILLY. You told me your name was Ramona.

RAYMOND. Actually, I said Raymond. You heard wrong.

BILLY. You never corrected me.

RAYMOND. I thought you were being cute. Funny. Trust me, I didn't think you were that dumb.

BILLY. Well, you were wrong!

RAYMOND. I know!

BILLY. You were.

RAYMOND. I know. And as soon as I realized I was, what did I do? I sent you home. Tried to spare you the embarrassment. I had no intention of ever seeing you again, but it was you who –

BILLY. Intention?

RAYMOND. – it was you who insisted we see each other. Even when I found your wallet, you were insistent. Don't mail it!

BILLY. I thought you were a girl.

RAYMOND. Come on, Billy.

BILLY. I did!

RAYMOND. Come on. We're making out on the couch. You're getting hard. I'm getting hard. It's serious dry humping cock on cock action and you think – what – this chick must have one really firm vagina? Come on!

BILLY breaks down sobbing.

RAYMOND. Oh, shit. Shit. I'm sorry.

BILLY. Don't...

RAYMOND. I didn't mean to scare you. I'm sorry for talking dirty. Sometimes I cross the line.

BILLY. *I* don't talk like that.

RAYMOND. Look. Billy, it's okay. Sex can be confusing. So we had fun for a few hours. You felt a spark, I felt a spark. It doesn't mean you're...

BILLY. I don't get it. What are you? Like a... trans... one of them, you know, where they snip off your...

RAYMOND. Transexual? No, Billy. I'm not a transexual.

BILLY. Then a... what? Where you like dressing up like a girl?

RAYMOND. Uh... no. Look, lemme make this easy for you. I'm an actor. *(sees* **BILLY** *still doesn't get it)* No? ...I auditioned for this pilot which I didn't get but the fag-haggy casting director liked me and asked if I do drag cuz her fucking stepbrother was opening up this club and like any good starving actor I lied, and the tips are great, so now I pay my rent by "becoming a woman" three hours a day, Wednesday thru Sunday. Rest of the time, I'm a man. It's a very specific uniform for a very specific job. Like what you're wearing.

BILLY. But I'm not a cop.

RAYMOND. And I'm not a woman.

BILLY. Then what are you?

RAYMOND. What are you?

> *BLACKOUT.* **[LIVING ROOM].** **OMAR** *and* **CHLOE** *by the fridge eating ice cream. She's in just a T-shirt, he's in just boxers. They've already settled into each other.*

CHLOE. Not that I *need* to have ice cream after sex, I'm just saying it completes the whole experience.

OMAR. First the rush of orgasm, then the –

CHLOE. Rush of sugar. Prolongs the night.

OMAR. Until the crash.

CHLOE. I like the crash.

OMAR. I love the crash. That's where you really get to sleep together. Nothing's better than the sleep.

CHLOE. So... you're staying?

OMAR. Why wouldn't I?

> **CHLOE** *smiles, kisses* **OMAR**. *It's passionate.*

CHLOE. You want to...

OMAR. Again?

CHLOE. Only if you want to.

> **OMAR** *runs upstairs. But* **CHLOE** *stays behind.*

OMAR. Um, this'll only work if we're both together.

CHLOE. I'll be right there. I just... wanna put the ice cream away.

> **OMAR** *exits. A moment of solitude for* **CHLOE**. *And as she puts the dessert away, she's hit by the power of her connection.*

MARK. *(entering again from upstairs)* Okay, this is just getting weird...

CHLOE. You scared me.

MARK. There Billy and I were in the jacuzzi, with the Lady-cops. One of them asks us what precinct we're from and I make up a number, I go: uh the 16th, and the other one goes Hey that's my brother's precinct, he's never mentioned you two! Nutty coincidence, right? Nutty, but not hopeless. Could've easily been saved with a "we're rookies" or whatever, but instead Billy goes, and this is the really weird part, Billy goes I'm sorry. I can't do this. We're *lying*. This is all just a scheme we made up to get into your pants and, uh, it's wrong. And he gets up and leaves. Just like that. I mean, that's pretty un-Billy, don't you think, to leave a perfect scene like that?

CHLOE. I don't know.

MARK. What do you mean you don't know?

CHLOE. I mean I don't –

MARK. So you don't think Billy –

CHLOE. I don't know, Mark. I don't know. I don't, and, and, I don't... care.

MARK. You don't –

CHLOE. Huh. Wow. I don't care.

MARK. But you're supposed to –

CHLOE. I don't care!

MARK. – you're supposed to care. That's what you do.

> **CONNOR** *(with luggage)* and **VERONICA** *(with Sunshine in the box)* enter the front door.

CONNOR. You'll really like the guest room. Let me know what time you want to get up.

As the two exit up the stairs:

VERONICA. Still hard to believe all six of you live here.

CONNOR. Yep. Six friends, eight rooms, one big penthouse in the Big Apple.

MARK. Wait. Veronica's back?

CHLOE. Guess so.

MARK. But, that doesn't – shouldn't she be done? Chloe, something's not right.

CHLOE. I know. Isn't it great?

MARK. No, it's not great. It's serious. It's very... *(he sees* **OMAR***'s jacket on a chair)* ...is he still here?

CHLOE. Who?

MARK. You know who.

CHLOE. He has a name, Mark.

MARK. Why is he still here?

CHLOE. That's none of your business.

MARK. This absolutely is my business. It's your *business*, too.

CHLOE. What I do on my own time is my (own) –

MARK. This is my penthouse.

CHLOE. Ours.

MARK. I heard what he said. Before.

CHLOE. You were watching us?

MARK. He's dangerous.

CHLOE. To who?

MARK. We don't know him.

CHLOE. *You* don't.

MARK. Look, I just –

CHLOE. No.

MARK. Chloe.

CHLOE. You're not taking this from me.

MARK. I'm trying to –

CHLOE. You always do.

MARK. I'm trying to understand why this is happening.

CHLOE. *What's* happening, Mark? Nothing! Nothing except Ladycops and porno Bar Mitzvah presents and schemes and neuroses and all the other crap that keeps us from, from –

MARK. From what?

CHLOE. – from thinking straight.

MARK. We don't need to think, Chloe, that's what I've (been) –

CHLOE. I'm suffocating here. Suffocating! Aren't you?

> **FIONA** *enters the front door with* **HARVEY**. **FIONA**: *hair up, glasses on, cigarette in hand. As they exit upstairs:*

FIONA. ...but I think for me what makes the book such a

great, um, social document is that shocking scene at the end where –

HARVEY. Where Rosasharn breast feeds the starving man. I know. It's, it's historical testimony at its best.

MARK. Now Harvey, too? You don't see anything odd about... A couple days ago everything was perfect! *We* were perfect.

CHLOE. We were? Because last I checked I still can't sleep, Connor's depressed, Stephanie's blocked and Billy...

MARK. Billy's fine!

Front door bursts open. It's **BILLY,** *with* **RAYMOND.** *They're making out, shedding each others clothes as they run up the stairs.*

MARK. What the hell? You see? You see! It's him!

CHLOE. Who?

MARK. It's gotta be. He's throwing everybody off!

CHLOE. Are you out (of) –

MARK. Chloe, your friend doesn't belong here.

CHLOE. Why him, Mark? Why isn't it any of the others? Harvey or Veronica or –

MARK. You know why.

CHLOE. – or that guy Billy was just kissing?

MARK. You were a different person when you came back from that play. I noticed. Something in you changed.

CHLOE. I should hope so.

MARK. He was there, wasn't he?

CHLOE. He has a name.

MARK. At the play. THREE SISTERS. He –

CHLOE. Has a name.

MARK. Omar. Was there.

CHLOE. Yes, Mark, Omar (was) –

MARK. Voodoo! He was there and he did it. He, he put something very dangerous in motion. Something he had no right to.

CHLOE. Voodoo?

MARK. Not voodoo. Desire.

CHLOE. Do you know how racist that is?

MARK. I'm the racist? You let this guy come in out of nowhere and sweep you off your feet and I'm the racist? So if this guy didn't look different, if he was like me –

CHLOE. White.

MARK. Yes, white! You really think you would have let him –

CHLOE. Of course.

MARK. You would have let him –

CHLOE. Oh my God.

MARK. You wouldn't have even looked at him. You're such a total coward in your own life that you have to –

CHLOE. Good night, Mark.

MARK. – you have to exoticize some guy off the street to...

He stops himself, caught up in his own emotion. The two stand before each other. The moment hangs. Then: **CHLOE** *heads up the stairs.* **MARK** *grabs her arm.*

CHLOE. Take your hand off me.

MARK. You're making a mistake.

CHLOE. *I love him.*

MARK. Because he's different.

CHLOE. Because he's real. From the world. He sees me. Listens. No affectation, no rug about to be swept out from under me, he's just... here. Who can you say that about, Mark? Who has *ever* reminded you about the things you always knew were there but never really saw?

MARK. Chloe, that kind of talk has no place here.

CHLOE. So terrorism?

MARK. Whoa.

CHLOE. Homelessness?

MARK. WHOA!

CHLOE. I didn't even know we were at war! I'm 36! How

pathetic is that? Thousands of people dead – on our end and theirs – but this is the first I've heard of it.

MARK. You really wanna bring all that in?

CHLOE. Why not? Maybe it's time we start addressing reality.

MARK. Reality is for the depressed and those without imagination.

CHLOE. Oh, and getting yourself into one silly situation week after week is better? Don't you want more?

MARK. Chloe.

CHLOE. Just a touch. A touch of what's real? Because this, all this, Mark, it doesn't seem so real to me. Not anymore.

She backs herself into the staircase banister, holding onto the spindles for support. She turns around to address **MARK**, *accidentally pulling one of the spindles off with her.*

Like this... it's not real.

She lifts up the coffee table. The magazines glued in place on it do not fall.

And this!

As she moves to the house phone:

MARK. Chloe, you need to calm down.

CHLOE. This phone? No cord, Mark. Not real! And this?

CHLOE *easily shoves the "locked" butcher block into the counter.*

Not real! Nothing is real! Nothing except the questions in my head. Questions like, like... pigeons! That's why I can't sleep. I've got pigeons in my head keeping me awake with their questions!

CHLOE *RUSHES the couch and flips it over.*

MARK. Chloe!

CHLOE. What does it mean? Why is there war? Will I die?

If I do, where will I go when I go? What if I've already gone?

With a yell, she CHARGES over to the kitchen wall flat and PUSHES it over, exposing the theatre – yes, your theatre – itself. **CONNOR, FIONA** *and* **BILLY** *enter. A new* **CHLOE** *looks to them.*

Maybe we're not even human. You know? Maybe we don't exist at all and I just think I'm walking and eating and PISSING and SHITTING and FUCKING AND IT'S ALL FOR FUCKING SHIT and if I could only see the questions – see them like Chekhov did – then maybe I could rest! So please, please let me see everything as it really, really is!

CHLOE *bangs on the door and – like a Buster Keaton stunt – the frame surrounding it COLLAPSES over her, making visible the theatre set's braces, glow tape, and more. Chest heaving,* **CHLOE** *looks to the destruction around her, to the artificial set that has been revealed.*

CHLOE. Let me see it all.

END OF ACT ONE

ACT TWO

[LIVING ROOM – 5 WEEKS LATER]. **MARK** *is hammering the fallen door frame back up as:* **CHLOE** *and* **FIONA** *read the paper and* **RAYMOND** *stretches before a run. Time passes. Desperate for attention,* **MARK** *tries to get anybody to notice him. Nobody does. So he pretends to hammer his thumb.*

MARK. Ow! Just hammered my thumb. I'm okay, though. All good.

FIONA. I'm done with this section if (you) –

CHLOE. One sec.

A tired **VERONICA** *enters from upstairs, and* **RAYMOND** *goes to get her coffee.*

RAYMOND. Hey, V.

FIONA. How's it going?

VERONICA. I don't know who's more stubborn, that dog or your brother.

FIONA. He's always been like that. Once Connor gets his mind set.

VERONICA. It's a lot of hard work, breaking a canine. And one that hates men? Forget it.

FIONA. Mm.

VERONICA. *(to* **RAYMOND** *as he exits)* Have a good run. *(to* **FIONA***)* It's been over a month. There's not much more I can do for him, you know? For either of them. Sunshine's still gonna bark, Connor's still gonna want him not to. And as my mentor once said, sometimes a fit's just not a fit.

FIONA. He's not a quitter. You're gonna have to push him to win or push him to walk.

VERONICA. Yeah, I thought I picked up on that.

MARK. Boring.

FIONA. Either way, Connor can handle it, but you gotta commit. *(hands her the paper)* Saved you the crossword.

VERONICA. Cheers.

MARK. Really boring!

He exits.

VERONICA. Any word from Steph?

FIONA. *(shrugs)* She's always been closer to Chloe. Hey. Chlo.

CHLOE. *(engrossed in the paper)* Hm?

FIONA. Any word from Steph?

CHLOE. Still camped out in her office, my guess. Working on the block. She'll come up for air soon.

VERONICA. It's been a while.

FIONA. That's nothing. She disappears every summer.

CHLOE. Speaking of, did you see they found that girl's body? So tragic. Almost as tragic as what those neighbors did to that guy in Levittown. Who sets people on fire? Oh, oh, and where was it, the high school girl who got suspended which, you know, as a Jew I can totally sympathize with.

FIONA. I didn't know you were Jewish.

CHLOE. Oh. Yeah. And not that I don't believe in God, I do, but separation of church and state. Very simple.

MARK. *(entering with the board game)* Who's up for the Pyramid?

CHLOE. And the thing is, y'know, there are all these stories are out there, right –

MARK. Ronnie, Fiona?

CHLOE. – but who decides what stories get told and what don't and why because, I mean, I don't get it, I look out my window and, unless I'm wrong, there is a lot that is *not* being told.

MARK. Brand new set of cards right here.

FIONA. No, you get it.

MARK. Play with me!

> **MARK** *exits. The women return to the paper – except for* **CHLOE**, *who keeps an eye on* **FIONA**. *A beat as Fiona senses* **CHLOE** *watching her.*

FIONA. What?

CHLOE. Okay, I know you don't want to talk about it, but... you haven't said anything.

FIONA. There's nothing to say.

CHLOE. So Harvey's really going?

FIONA. Taxi'll be here any minute.

VERONICA. That's today? Aw, babe, are you... ?

FIONA. Okay? No. I finally meet a guy and. What am I supposed to... He knew what he was getting himself into. So did I.

CHLOE. Maybe there's something we can do.

FIONA. Chloe, it's the reserves.

CHLOE. We could stage a protest. Get them to listen.

> **FIONA** *goes to get more coffee as* **MARK** *returns to fix the broken banister spindle.*

FIONA. Sweetie, no offense, but protesting is dead. This is the new millennium, where the will of the people has been put on block sender.

OMAR. *(entering; gets coffee)* Morning.

CHLOE. Come on, that's too cynical, even for you. You can't dismiss it, not *all* of it. It's gotta count for something.

VERONICA. *(filling* **OMAR** *in)* Protesting.

OMAR.
Mm.

(HARVEY, in uniform, enters)
Morning. Coffee?

(HARVEY nods, goes to kiss FIONA.)

CHLOE.
Look at what the, the hippies did during Viet Nam, right? That war was going on forever and they kept protesting, and it took a while, but it worked. I mean, they were heard. They ended the war.

FIONA. The war didn't end because hippies protested, the war ended because we were losing.

CHLOE. Okay, maybe not protesting alone, but –

FIONA. That's the truth.

CHLOE. So they had no influence?

FIONA. Not none. They made good TV.

CHLOE. Then what's the – I mean, this is gonna sound whatever – but what's the point of having a democracy if we don't have any say?

HARVEY.
We have a say. We're not silenced. We're not China.

MARK.
(hammers thumb again)
Ow!

FIONA. No, but close.

HARVEY. We have to acknowledge the fact that we vote for a president, for a congress –

FIONA. Fair enough.

HARVEY. – so we have a say.

OMAR. Some. Some have a say.

MARK. *(exiting)* Yawn!

FIONA. That's what I'm getting at. That the governments that are elected are made up of rich, white guys –

OMAR. Thank you.

FIONA. – who have a vested interest in protecting their assets, whatever those assets may be.

CHLOE. So why –

HARVEY. That's ridiculous...

CHLOE.

Why can't we just vote them out?

FIONA.

And replace them with who?

CHLOE.

I don't know, somebody who, right, who cares. Or whatever, somebody who won't exploit the system.

FIONA.

It's not that simple.

CHLOE.

I mean, isn't that the, uh, the principle this country is based on?

FIONA.

But it takes money to –

CHLOE.

Anybody can run.

FIONA.

But you can't have a campaign without –

CHLOE.

A government for the people by the people.

HARVEY.

...all kinds of different people make up the face of government.

OMAR.

Yeah, but it's mostly what Fiona says, you know, it's these guys and they decide who gets heard and who doesn't.

HARVEY.

And that's why there's checks and balances in place.

OMAR.

The media's guilty of the same thing. Look at what passes for "news" these days: does it reflect real reality or is it an interpretation of reality and if so, who's doing the interpreting?

HARVEY.

Well, obviously it's blind black lesbians.

OMAR.

In wheelchairs.

FIONA. That's just not reality. Use your brain, Chloe. Who has the kind of money it takes to run an effective campaign?

HARVEY. Fi.

CHLOE. No, I know what you're saying, but –

FIONA. What *poor person* has the money to run?

HARVEY. Okay, Fi.

FIONA. No. Or can take time off work, you know, to head a campaign? You've gotta get signatures and shake hands and make phone calls. Most "for-the-people-by-the-people" people take a sick day and they're out on the street.

CHLOE. That's where you get friends and family and people who believe in your message to help out. Grass roots.

FIONA. Then go. Be grass roots. Do your thing. Stop volunteering at the homeless shelter and see how far (you) –

CHLOE. Oh, shit! I totally forgot I told Helen I'd get these clothes to her by noon.

Getting her coat and the bag of clothing by the door:

OMAR. Want me to come with?

CHLOE. Nah, I gotta take the sixth up to the South Bronx after. Remember? Neil's committing his mother today and he needs me to cover the phones?

OMAR. Right.

CHLOE. Besides, you should get some rest. The way you were tossing and turning last night...

OMAR. You noticed?

CHLOE. Hard not to.

*She kisses **OMAR** goodbye. Then turns to hug **HARVEY** with:*

CHLOE. You'll probably be gone by the time I...

HARVEY. *(re: **FIONA**)* She won't let you, but take care of her anyway.

CHLOE *exits as **BILLY** descends the stairs.*

BILLY. Oh good, you're still here.

HARVEY. How'd it go last night?

BILLY. Don't ask.

CONNOR (O.S.). Veronica!

VERONICA. What was last night?

FIONA. Raymond stayed over.

VERONICA. Again? That's great.

BILLY. Harvey's been, you know, helping me with...

HARVEY. Just advising.

BILLY. ...advising me with... oh God, he hates me. My boyfriend hates me.

CONNOR (O.S.). Veronica!

BILLY. *(as* **VERONICA** *exits)* I can't blame him. I used to dump girls for a lot less. Don't sleep with me on date number one, you're out. And this is... I mean, I've stopped counting.

FIONA. Billy.

BILLY. He's really patient. He just wants to get closer. That's all. He wants to get closer and I can't...

HARVEY. I thought we talked about at least letting him give you a blow job.

BILLY. I did. Twice. But whatever, that's like hand-holding to these guys.

FIONA. What about you? Did you blow him back?

BILLY. I just got used to letting him put his tongue in my mouth. Now I'm supposed to –

HARVEY. Of course, you're supposed to.

BILLY. Have you?

HARVEY. *(looking to his Navy uniform)* Not telling.

BILLY. He keeps talking about how hot I am. How I turn him on. And, you know, specifics – like dirty words and all – about what he wants us to do together, y'know, when I'm ready. Stuff I never even did with girls, cuz, right, I didn't even know you could put that there.

HARVEY. It's pillow talk, Billy. I told you about that. Some people use dirty words when they fool around. What did he say?

BILLY. Stuff. Just stuff.

HARVEY. We're all adults here. Maybe if you say the words out loud, we can talk about them and they won't seem so... bizarre.

BILLY. It's private.

FIONA. Did he say he wanted to have anal sex?

A hyped-up **MARK** *enters in a gray wig and a matronly dress. He's got other gray wigs with him.*

MARK. Oh-ho-okay, who wants to see Hootie & the Blow-fish? They're doing a benefit at the old folks home tonight!

BILLY. He didn't say that exactly.

MARK. C'mon, let's dress up like senile old grandmas!

HARVEY. Did he say he wanted you to fuck him?

BILLY. Can you not use the –

HARVEY. Sorry.

BILLY. – that word?

HARVEY. My bad. Not fuck. Do.

MARK. Come on, this is Hootie, folks!

FIONA. Mark! Are you gonna keep doing this because it's really fucking annoying!

MARK *takes off his wig, exits.*

HARVEY. So... about Raymond.

FIONA. Did he say he wanted you to do him?

BILLY. Kinda.

HARVEY. Ohhh, I think I understand. Raymond wants to do *you*. Am I right?

BILLY. He wants to get close.

FIONA. And I always pegged him as a pushy bottom.

HARVEY. How do you feel, Billy? Do you want to get close to Raymond in the way that Raymond wants to get close to you?

BILLY. I don't know. You guys know how much I like him. I mean, we're having a kickass time together. I haven't felt like this with anybody. And I do, I want to, I want to have sex, make love with him so bad... but every time we start it's just... it's like... I can't shut my brain off.

OMAR. What's it saying? *(beat)* Billy, what's your brain saying?

BILLY. ...You don't know what you're doing. You look like an idiot. Don't just lie there, do something. Jesus, you're awkward. And clumsy. Get ready, he's gonna laugh at you – here. No, here. Here. Quit shaking, dummy. Don't let go.

HARVEY. You're feeling vulnerable. That's a good thing.

BILLY. I feel like I'm dying.

FIONA. Maybe... have you tried having a couple beers first?

HARVEY. Just to relax. Or a scotch.

BILLY. But I don't want to be on anything. This is important to me.

HARVEY. All I'm saying is –

FIONA. All he's saying is if you don't experiment, sexually or otherwise, you'll never grow.

HARVEY. And that's what this is all about, isn't it? Your own maturation? I mean if (you) –

Taxi HORN HONKS. Everyone is still. A beat as **HARVEY** *goes to hug* **FIONA** *goodbye, but instead...*

FIONA. I'll see ya.

*...***FIONA** *runs upstairs. No kiss, no hug.* **HARVEY***'s alone. To* **BILLY** *and* **OMAR***:*

HARVEY. It's okay. I had it coming.

HARVEY *hugs them both, exits. A beat as* **BILLY** *goes to get a drink, and* **OMAR** *has something to confess.*

OMAR. You wanna know what my brain is saying? That I'm in love with Chloe. Took me 34 years to find her, but I did. And it's the real thing, Billy, you know, and I think, when you're as lucky as you and me to find the real thing, you, um, you start asking yourself if you deserve it. And you may not feel like you do, so you – self-fulfilling prophecy, right – you do something stupid to sabotage it.

BILLY. Like not making love even though I want to?

OMAR. Maybe we just have to remind ourselves that as much as we're scared... they're scared, too.

RAYMOND. *(entering from the front door)* Whooo!

BILLY. How was your run?

RAYMOND. Short. It's bitter out there.

BILLY. Where you going?

RAYMOND. Shower.

BILLY. Wait up. I'll come with.

> BILLY *smiles to* OMAR, *exits upstairs. Once he's gone,* OMAR *starts clearing coffee mugs. And* MARK *enters to clean up the living room.*

MARK. Hey, sorry for interrupting back there. I just really thought you'd wanna take in a final concert before you left.

OMAR. We're out of dish soap.

MARK. It's okay, buddy. I know what you're up to.

OMAR. I'm not up to anything.

MARK. Right.

OMAR. Mark, do you have a problem with me?

MARK. Do I have a problem with you? No, I don't. But Chloe does. Or she will, lemme put it that way.

OMAR. So we're being cryptic now. Why don't you tell me what's on your mind.

MARK. I'd rather not. Let's just say that the savior ain't looking so savory.

OMAR. *(heading upstairs)* Grow up.

MARK. Best of luck in Berkeley. What time are you leaving tomorrow? You should hit the road early. It's a five day drive and you'll want to make good time, so...

OMAR. ...How did you find out?

MARK. Grandma Shirley always said these walls were thin.

OMAR. So you know about the teaching position.

MARK. Tenure track, good for you, dawg. What time do you pick up the U-HAUL?

OMAR. Shit.

MARK. Yeah, shit. So tell me, you think Chloe will have a

problem with you disappearing, just like that? Or were you planning on telling her some time tonight? Maybe give her a good eight hours notice before ripping her heart out and leaving me clean up the mess?

OMAR. You really should keep your nose out of people's business.

MARK. "Hey, Chlo, it's Omie. I's got good news and I's got bad news."

OMAR. I wouldn't.

MARK. "I'll give you the bad news first. I'm taking off for Californy tomorrow and you'll never see me again. Now the good news, and you'll like this, the good news is I'm gonna get busy with you one last time – "

OMAR *CHARGES* **MARK** *against the banister.*

Ooh, truth hurts. And it plays right into your dissertation. Which would make you, what, both a liar *and* a cliche.

OMAR *puts* **MARK** *in a chokehold.*

OMAR. Truth? Truth: she loves *me*, Mark. I got the girl. You didn't!

OMAR *releases* **MARK,** *runs out. BLACK OUT. LIGHTS on* **[STEPHANIE'S OFFICE]***, littered with empty takeout containers and coffee cups.* **STEPHANIE** *hasn't changed or bathed in five weeks. She wears a phone headset, pacing back and forth until:*

STEPHANIE. Hello? HellohMYGODhello! I've been on hold so long I wasn't sure if I got disconnected but I don't think I did if this is you, LaVyrle, IS this you, LaVyrle, do you mind if I call you LaVyrle? Um, oh, it's me, Ms. Spencer: Stephanie Dash. No-no-no-no, don't hang up! I know I shouldn't be calling you at home, but I got your number from – well, I don't want to get anybody fired – just please. I, I don't know how much your cleaning lady told you, but I'm a romance novelist like you – okay, not like you, I don't have 15 million

copies in print or a deal with Lifetime – yet, hahaha –
BUT. *(breaks down)* I'm blocked, Ms. Spencer. I've been
in this office for 41 days straight and haven't written
a word, stuck in the same scene I've been trying to
get through for over a year. It's this scene, this scene
where my leading lady, a cool modern businesswoman,
right, has been dating this guy, Tom, who she met at
this charity event, and everybody loves Tom because
he's Tom, quirky loveable helpful Tom, who just asked
her to marry him but, the thing is, she won't say yes. I
mean, she's supposed to. To say yes. Otherwise I have
no story. But. Every time I type it out, Y-E-S, it comes
out N-O! N-O! Like my fingers won't let me type it cuz
it's not true to the character, y'know? And he's not
bad, this guy, Connor, I mean Tom, it's just, I think
my lead gets that he's not right for her. Y'know? So
she won't let me type Y-E-S, cuz whenever she's around
Connor-Tom-Fuck he turns her into this thing that
she's not – controlling and mean and naggy – and
I'm sure Connor doesn't mean to do it but he does
and I don't hate my husband, I don't, but I hate the
person that I am with him, y'know, the person that I've
become and I swear to you I'm not that person, I'm
not an asshole but what am I supposed to do, LaVyrle?
Because I'm not giving up on Love. I write about Love.
I need Love. And if give that up, if I give up Love... I
have no husband, no marriage, no career, and then
what? What am I left with? What the fuck do I have
then, LaVyrle?

BLACK OUT. **[LIVING ROOM – LATER].** **OMAR**'s
*on the couch, waiting for the door to open. It does. A
freezing* **CHLOE** *enters. She's not wearing a coat or
sweater or shoes.*

CHLOE. It's not what you think.

OMAR.	**CHLOE.**
My God.	I'm fine, I just... can we go?

OMAR. You're freezing. What happened to your –

CHLOE. Can we just please get out of here?

OMAR. *(covering her with a blanket)* Chloe, what happened?

CHLOE. I don't know. I mean, I was on the train. Sitting across from this woman – our age, maybe a little older – she's wearing this paper thin windbreaker, no gloves, broken shoes. I ask her where she's going. She says work. Six dollars an hour. I just had to.

OMAR. Had to what?

CHLOE. I can get new clothes. She can't.

OMAR. You gave her your clothes?

CHLOE. I gave her as much as I could until she was like, uh, okay crazy lady, that's enough. But I don't feel like it was enough. It's fine shuttling food, answering calls here and there, but... I want to give more, be in the world more. These women I volunteer with, Molly and Dina, they know this AIDS hospice on the west coast that's looking for help.

OMAR. Chloe, slow down.

CHLOE. I can't. If I do, I'll change my mind.

OMAR. What about your friends?

CHLOE. They'll understand.

OMAR. And your curtain business? It took you six years to –

CHLOE. I don't care.

OMAR. I'm just saying it... seems kinda drastic.

CHLOE. It is drastic! It should be drastic. This is how lives are altered, Omar. You make a bold choice, a crazy choice, and you stick with it. You were a graphic designer before you –

OMAR. You're right.

CHLOE. – before you moved into film theory, you know that more than –

OMAR. I said you're right.

CHLOE. – more than anybody. I need a change and I can't do it here. Not in this city, not in this goddamn apartment where everything is familiar. I need to scare myself shitless. I need to get out of here so I can be free of... me.

OMAR. So where are on the coast are these clinics?

CHLOE. San Francisco. We could leave tonight. We could drive across the country and see America before we start a brand new life together. Does that sound like something you could be a part of? *(no response)* ...What?

OMAR. *(hesitating to tell her, then:)* I was gonna leave you. There's this job at UC Berkeley. I've had it since before we met and I never told you about it because... I never expected this to... but we, you know, we kept getting better and better and each day it got harder to tell you I've got this job and I'm leaving soon. So I packed up a U-Haul and I was just gonna write a note and cut out, slip away tomorrow morning and never look back.

CHLOE. What happened?

OMAR. I couldn't leave you. So I – here's the funny part – I called up the Dean and told him I wouldn't be taking the job.

CHLOE *hands him a slip of paper.*

What's this?

CHLOE. Confirmation slip for the U-HAUL. It fell out of your coat.

OMAR. You knew?

CHLOE. Why didn't you just ask me to go with?

OMAR. I didn't think you'd say yes. In case you hadn't noticed, I'm a little... I'm far from perfect. That's just me. Sometimes I do, I get scared and I make mistakes. Does that sound like something *you* could be part of?

BLACKOUT. SOUNDS of a dog WHIMPERING as LIGHTS UP on **[CONNOR'S BEDROOM]. CON-NOR***'s kneeling by the box, whispering to Sunshine. As* **VERONICA** *coaches:*

VERONICA. Good. That's it, Connor. He's really responding. Okay now, last attempt. Pick up your puppy.

CONNOR goes to pick the dog up. It seems like it's going to happen. But NO. The dog BARKS like never before. Over it:

CONNOR. Dammit!

VERONICA. *(picking up the box)* That's it, then.

CONNOR. Wait, no, you –

VERONICA. We had a deal. It didn't work out, it's time for us to go.

CONNOR. *(tries to take box)* I'm about to break through, I know it!

VERONICA. Connor.

CONNOR. No, no! Come on, Sunshine! Please be a good boy and let me shush you. Let me tell you once again how it's a good thing to be a man and really hear me this time, okay (because) –

VERONICA. *(heading to door with box)* Connor!

CONNOR. – because I am seriously about to lose it. In fact I'm done. I'M DONE SHUSHING. Maybe I should, I dunno, SCREAM in your face SHUT THE FUCK UP, maybe if I bark louder than you, you stupid fucking piece of dogshit, maybe then I'll get through! Huh? HUH?!

The barking STOPS. CONNOR looks to VERONICA. VERONICA puts the box down.

Oh, so that's it? You think if you bark at me I'll go away and you'll never have to deal with another man again? Well, fuck you, Sunshine! Yeah, fuck you, because like it or not, you are more of a man than me.

As VERONICA quietly exits:

Only a man barks loud enough so he doesn't have to hear what is good about him. Only a man barks so he can drown out the good stuff and can go on believing what's been drilled into his brain ever since he was a boy in diapers: that all men, not some but all men are wife beaters and deadbeat dads and lazy husbands and corrupt leaders and brutal rapists and drug pushers and felons, pedophiles, homos, cheapskates, losers, animals. Take your daughter to work day, leave your stupid hopeless pathetic son behind. A woman she gives life, but a man, a man will undoubtedly take it away. Is that what you need to hear, Sunshine? That all a man does is destroy? Because if that's the case, then we should just end it. Together, you and me. Two men who finally discover the truth decide, in a grand, self-less gesture, to help out society by doing themselves in. Because good or bad, you really want to know what it means to be a man, Sunshine? To be a man means to, every day, in small, silent imperceptible ways, to be a man means... to kill yourself.

BLACKOUT. LIGHTS UP on **[THE KITCHEN]** *where the refrigerator door casts a light on* **BILLY,** *who's in his underwear eating ice cream.* **RAYMOND** *turns on the lights and descends the stairs. He's dressed, carrying a garment bag for the night. Kissing* **BILLY:**

RAYMOND. Gotta go. Show's at seven. Don't wanna be late.

BILLY. You have everything?

RAYMOND. All set. Hey, sorry I can't make the dinner. I know it's important to you. To me, too. I just –

BILLY. No, I know. I mean, it'd be great for you to be there, but there'll be other times for us to – whatever. We're good. So what time you think you'll be back?

RAYMOND. I'm not sure. Remember, I'm subbing for Lady Velour tonight?

BILLY. Oh, right.

RAYMOND. It's like two shows back to back. I'll be going really late. I'm thinking I'll just crash at my place.

BILLY. Oh, okay. So I'll let myself in.

RAYMOND. *(making a face)* Mmm...

BILLY. Or not.

RAYMOND. I've got that commercial audition in the morning...

BILLY. Oh. Right.

RAYMOND. It's no big deal. I just really should get some sleep. Even for a little.

BILLY. Sure.

RAYMOND. It's a crazy night, that's all. Okay?

BILLY. Sure. *(then:)* Did I do something? Because if I did, we should, you know, it's okay to talk about it.

RAYMOND. Oh, Billy. Please don't read into this. Please. I like being with you and I'm looking forward to seeing where this goes. Really. I promise I'll call you later, okay?

BILLY. Forget it. Don't worry about it.

RAYMOND. No, I will. I'll call (you) –

BILLY. I said don't worry about it. Just take your shit and go.

RAYMOND. Now you're being defensive.

BILLY. And you're being an asshole.

RAYMOND. How am I being an asshole?

BILLY. You know how.

RAYMOND. No, I don't. I'm not a mind reader.

BILLY. I didn't say you were.

RAYMOND. What? Is this because of the dinner? Sleeping over?

BILLY. Forget it.

RAYMOND. Billy, I have to go. I'm gonna be late.

BILLY. So go. *(pushing* **RAYMOND** *away; hard)* GO!

> **RAYMOND** *exits. Meanwhile,* **VERONICA***'s been standing on the stairs, luggage in hand, looking for a good time to descend.*

VERONICA. Hey. Is everything all right?

BILLY. *(pulling it together)* ...Yeah, sure. You leaving?

VERONICA. Yup. Believe it or not, my work here is done.

BILLY. So, the dog's okay now? He's cured?

VERONICA. Don't know about cured, but Sunshine and Connor have finally bonded. I think they'll fit together quite well from now on.

BILLY. That's great. Just... terrific. Hey, we should celebrate.

VERONICA. I'd love to but the taxi's on its way.

BILLY. Come on. We'll have a beer.

VERONICA. I really should get going.

BILLY. One beer. It's Foster's.

VERONICA. I hate Foster's.

BILLY. Good, cause I lied. Heineken?

VERONICA. All right, one beer. But as soon as the doorman gives a ring, I'm off.

BILLY. Fair enough. Okay, a toast. A toast to... a job well done.

VERONICA. To a job well done.

BILLY. And to Sunshine.

VERONICA. To Sunshine.

> **BILLY** *accidentally/on purpose spills some beer down his chest. naked chest. It's embarrassingly not subtle.*

BILLY. Oops.

VERONICA. Careful.

> **VERONICA** *smiles awkwardly.* **OMAR** *enters from upstairs; he's carrying a balled up shirt.*

OMAR. Billy. Where's the, uh, the iron?

BILLY. Laundry room.

OMAR. *(as he exits)* You better get dressed.

BILLY. Can I just say, cuz I probably haven't said it before, it's been really nice having you here. You're so, like... international.

VERONICA. Thanks. To tell you the truth, it's been really nice being here. Shooting on location can get real lonely real quick; I'll take this over a fancy hotel room any day. Such a relief to be around real people. Especially the girl people. No offense.

BILLY. Not many women in your industry, huh?

VERONICA. You don't know how many times I've had cramps on the set and the grips, camera guys, they don't get it.

BILLY. We don't, do we?

BILLY sees this as his cue. Moving closer to her:

VERONICA. Billy.

BILLY. You smell nice.

VERONICA. This isn't a good idea.

BILLY. I can do this.

VERONICA. You're embarrassing yourself.

BILLY. Come on.

VERONICA. I'm serious.

BILLY. Me, too, baby. Just relax.

He holds her forcefully. It's tense.

VERONICA. Billy. What are you –

A struggle. A serious one. It's gotten real bad, real quick. But then, with a...

NO!

...VERONICA kicks BILLY in the nads. He goes down.

VERONICA. Are you fucking kidding me?!

With that, VERONICA grabs her bag and storms off. And BILLY is a complete mess, sobbing on the floor as MARK enters in his paramedics uniform.

MARK. Aw, jeez. Nice, William.

MARK turns around, opens up his gym bag, pulls out some clothes for BILLY.

MARK. Let's get some clothes on. Here. (*starts dressing BILLY*) Come on. Right leg first.

BILLY. Why do I feel this way?

MARK. Because you let yourself. Right leg.

BILLY. Harvey always said love should feel good.

MARK. Come on. Left leg.

BILLY. I'm a pussy.

MARK. You're not. You're Billy Tanner from Chippewa Falls, Wisconsin. You're a successful model, you just got your GED. Right? Now pull yourself together.

BILLY. You don't know about love.

MARK. I know plenty.

BILLY. Like what?

MARK. Arms. I know it's not always what it appears to be. I know it leaves people hurt instead of happy.

BILLY. How can you say that? Look at Chloe. She's unbelievable ever since Omar came –

MARK. Omar? You want to know the truth about Omar? He's got a teaching gig in Berkeley, he's leaving tomorrow, and he's not taking Chloe with him. And what's worse, he hasn't even told her yet.

BILLY. Don't be an idiot. Chloe knows.

MARK. No she doesn't.

BILLY. Yes she does. She's going with him. They're leaving tonight.

MARK. That's ridiculous. Chloe would tell me if she was –

BILLY. You really think Omar would just leave her behind? They're in love, Mark. That's what people in love do!

MARK. Why wouldn't Chloe tell me she's leaving?

BILLY. Maybe the same reason she didn't invite you to go out to dinner.

MARK. What dinner?

BILLY. The dinner where we all celebrate their move out west. The dinner you're not invited to because you don't know about love. Not like me and Chloe.

FIONA *comes downstairs.*

MARK. Well, don't you look nice. Where are you going?

FIONA. I thought you had work.

MARK. Soon. Where you going?

FIONA. Nowhere.

MARK. Dressed like that?

FIONA. ...A lecture.

MARK. Ooh, a little brain massage. What's it on?

FIONA. Hm?

MARK. The lecture. What's it on?

FIONA. Uh, this journalist who's been doing war coverage for The New Yorker is lecturing at Columbia, and we're –

BILLY. I told him.

FIONA. Billy, fuck. *(to* **MARK***)* You're not supposed to know until after Chloe's gone, okay? After. Promise me you won't ruin this evening.

MARK. Gee, I dunno. I gotta be able to experiment, otherwise I'll never really grow.

FIONA. I'm serious. This dinner means a lot to the both of them, so don't do anything stupid.

MARK. Dinner? You mean you were *lying* about the lecture? You're really going out for a nice meal instead? Wow. I mean, sure people lie in "the real world", too, but still, that's so... farcical of you. Guess old habits die hard.

BILLY. Mark.

MARK. I've been known to eat at restaurants, maybe I can come with.

FIONA. You're not invited.

MARK. Why? Because I wanted to play the Pyramid? See Hootie & the Blowfish?

FIONA. Because you're an asshole! You've always been an asshole and the truth is none of us ever liked you.

MARK. But, then why...

FIONA. Because you have a killer apartment.

The truth hits **MARK.** *A beat, then:*

BILLY. We better get going or we'll lose the reservation.

FIONA. Chloe! Connor! Come on!

A tear-streaked **STEPHANIE** *enters the front door, heading for the stairs.*

STEPHANIE. Is he up here?

FIONA. Oh my God.

BILLY. What happened to you?

STEPHANIE. *(calling up to him)* Connor! Is he up here?

FIONA. He'll be right down. Sweetie, you look awful. Are you – have you eaten? Do you want to (sit) –

STEPHANIE. Connor!

CONNOR. Stop shouting, I'm here.

> **CONNOR** *descends the stairs, sluggish and woozy. He's also carrying a plastic GAP bag in his hand. Something bulky is inside it.*

STEPHANIE. Connor.

CONNOR. Hey, babe. I missed you.

As he goes to throw the bag in the trash:

STEPHANIE. Listen, Connor, I gotta – Con.

CONNOR. Hey... you look great. Ooo, it's a liddle hot in here. How was your, um, you get any writing done?

STEPHANIE. No. We need to talk, can (we) –

CONNOR. Aw, baby. I thought you were gonna... gonna stay till you worked through your writing, um, the... god it's hot.

STEPHANIE. I was. I came back because I have something to tell you.

BILLY. Do you smell that?

STEPHANIE.	**FIONA.**
Are you okay?	Con?

CONNOR. I'm fine! I just gotta sit. Can I fucking sit down without you burrowing up my ass?

> **CHLOE** *appears at the railing, in a towel.*

CHLOE. Don't kill me.

FIONA. Chloe!

CHLOE. I know, I know. I'm sorry.

FIONA. We're gonna be late.

CHLOE. I'm almost there. Five minutes.

MARK. You better hurry. Don't want to miss the...

FIONA. Mark!

MARK. ...lecture.

BILLY. What is that?

> **CHLOE** *exits as* **BILLY** *heads over to the trash.*

MARK. See? I can play nice. I'm a team player.

FIONA. That's not funny.

STEPHANIE. I want a divorce.

BILLY. *(opening the GAP bag)* Oh Jesus!

> **BILLY** *drops the bag to the floor. Everybody stops.* **FIONA**
> *will go over next.*

BILLY. Sunshine.

CONNOR. *(re:* **STEPHANIE***)* What did she say?

BILLY. How could you?

FIONA. Oh my God. Con.

STEPHANIE. What?

> **STEPHANIE** *heads over to look. Then* **MARK**.

MARK. Yow. Nice work.

STEPHANIE. Shit! What the fuck?

BILLY. He was just a puppy.

CONNOR. I don't feel so good.

STEPHANIE. Are you on something?

CONNOR. No.

STEPHANIE. Con!

CONNOR. Maybe pills.

STEPHANIE. Pills?

FIONA. What pills?

> *Connor throws the pill bottle to* **BILLY**.

BILLY. Reglan?

MARK. *(laughing)* Oh, man.

CONNOR. I'm leaking.

> **CONNOR**'s *nipples have started leaking fluid.*

FIONA. You took my Reglan?

STEPHANIE. What's Reglan?

CONNOR. Why am I leaking?

FIONA. How much did you take?

STEPHANIE. What's Reglan?

BILLY. I'm gonna be sick.

FIONA. Con, how much did you take?

> **CONNOR**'s *nipples are now leaking even more fluid.*

CONNOR. I don't know, I don't know... one, two...

FIONA. That's it?

CONNOR. ...months supply. Two months supply. Yeah.

FIONA. Shit.

STEPHANIE. Would somebody please tell me what the fuck Reglan is!

MARK. It's a breast milk inducer.

STEPHANIE. A what?

MARK. A breast milk inducer. It's mainly for new moms who are low on milk supply, but some adoptive moms use it to force themselves to lactate.

BILLY. But, Fiona, you don't have a baby, why would (you) –

MARK. Oh, it's huge in the fetish community. Girls get to nurse the guys, it's a whole back-to-mama fantasy thing. There's a name for it. What's it called? Oh, yeah, suckling.

STEPHANIE. You and your fucking GRAPES OF WRATH!

FIONA. I am so sorry!

STEPHANIE. Con, come on, we're gonna get you to the hospital. Put your coat on.

CONNOR. No coat. Couch. Lie down.

STEPHANIE. No, no lying down.

BILLY. He was just a puppy.

> **CONNOR** *drops to the floor, starts having a seizure.*
> **FIONA, STEPHANIE** *and* **BILLY** *try to hold him down.*
> *It doesn't work.*

STEPHANIE. Con?

FIONA. Oh, shit.

STEPHANIE. What's going on?

FIONA. Mark!

MARK. *(casual)* Yuh, hun?

FIONA. Help!

MARK. Oh, so now I'm invited to the party?

BILLY. Easy, Con.

STEPHANIE. Please.

FIONA.	**STEPHANIE.**
Mark, you're the only one who knows what to do!	Help him!

> **CONNOR** *continues to thrash as* **MARK** *considers…*
> *then grabs a cushion from the couch and places it under*
> **CONNOR**'s *head.*

MARK. Everybody back off!

> *He loosens* **CONNOR**'s *tie, tips him on his side, jams his*
> *wallet in Connor's mouth to stop him from choking. As*
> **CONNOR** *calms…*

Go ahead and hate me all you want. I was protecting you. I was the only one who understood from the start the consequences of *him* being here. But no, you had to see it for yourselves. And worse, you're all set to let him take Chloe 3,000 miles away, even though you know if she goes it's the beginning of the end for us. What we have here is sacred and needs to be preserved, and you want to piss it all away. And for what? A taste of Reality? Well, how's that working out for you? Fiona? Steph? Was it worth it? Billy? Five weeks and look at what the world's already done to you.

*CONNOR's stopped seizing. He's resting. **MARK** points to the walls of the sitcom-like set surrounding everyone.*

This... is home. We're happy here. We're safe here. We're safe.

BILLY. Say you're right... what can we do about it now? We can't just go back to being the way we were, you know, and pretend we don't know what we already know.

*MARK cocks his head: sure you can. A long silence. One by one, they each nod to **MARK**. A pact is being made.*

STEPHANIE. What about Chloe?

MARK. I'll handle Chloe.

FIONA. (*exiting*) I'll get the car.

CONNOR. (*coming to*) We going for a ride?

STEPHANIE. No, Connor. We're going to the hospital.

CONNOR. Why? What happened?

*As **BILLY, CONNOR** and **STEPHANIE** head out:*

MARK. Steph, wait. I need to talk to you.

STEPHANIE. Mark, I gotta go.

MARK. He'll be okay. You'll catch up.

STEPHANIE. It can't wait?

MARK. They'll take care of him. I just need you for one minute.

STEPHANIE. Mark, he's my husband. I can't (just) –

MARK. Oh? Is that what he is, your husband? Because just a second ago I thought I heard you say something about a divorce.

STEPHANIE. Okay, okay. What do you want?

MARK. I want you to write a letter.

STEPHANIE. Now?

MARK. Yes.

STEPHANIE. You're joking, right?

MARK. Not at all.

STEPHANIE. Mark, I'm blocked, I haven't written anything for –

MARK. Bitch and moan, bitch and goddamn moan. Christ, Stephanie. You're not a writer.

STEPHANIE. I am, too.

MARK. No, you're not. A real writer has the sack to work through a block –

STEPHANIE. That's what I've been (doing) –

MARK. She'll take a pen, a piece of paper and force herself to write anything.

STEPHANIE. I tried that. I was holed up in that office for 41 days and I couldn't write a word because I –

MARK. You've fallen out of love. Yeah, yeah. You used that same excuse in college, same excuse in grad school.

STEPHANIE. Well, it's... true.

MARK. What the hell does love have to do with writing? Writing is craft. Cause and effect. Just admit it, Steph: the reason you can't write is because you don't *want* to write, because what you really want is to complain. Because you're a hack. A crybaby fucking hack.

STEPHANIE. *(a beat, then:)* What am I writing?

MARK. A Dear John letter.

STEPHANIE. That's it?

MARK. From Omar to Chloe.

STEPHANIE. Okay, so Omar's dumping Chloe. What else?

MARK. That's it. Make sure you put it in his handwriting. Write like a guy. Stay away from those girly swoops.

STEPHANIE. Gotcha. Now shut up, go away, and when you return, we'll see who's a fucking hack.

> **STEPHANIE** *writes* **OMAR**'s *letter while* **MARK** *searches for something. He ends up at the closet, pulls out the telescope Bar Mitzvah present. That looks heavy enough. He then heads offstage to the laundry room, while* **STEPHA-NIE** *gets into writing the letter. So into it, in fact, that she doesn't notice* **MARK** *returning, dragging a bloodied, knocked-out* **OMAR** *over to the balcony with him. As* **MARK** *opens the balcony door and shoves the wounded* **OMAR** *outside to the bitter cold:*

STEPHANIE. Hello! It's like freezing, shut the fucking door!

MARK shuts the door, draws the curtains, and heads over to STEPHANIE. Standing over her shoulder:

STEPHANIE. Wait. ...Okay. Done.

She gives the letter to MARK. As he reads:

I was kinda going for an it's-me-not-you sorta thing.

MARK. ...You, my dear, are a genius.

STEPHANIE. Well, I just... you put yourself inside the character's head and watch them destroy things. It's...

MARK. Easy.

STEPHANIE. Oh my God, I can write! I'm back! (*then:*) I gotta get to the hospital.

MARK. Hold up. I just need you for one more thing.

STEPHANIE. What's that?

CHLOE descends the stairs.

MARK. Credibility.

CHLOE. Hey. Where'd everybody go?

MARK. You better sit.

CHLOE. Can't. I gotta go to (this) –

STEPHANIE. Chloe.

CHLOE. What's going on?

MARK. Stephanie found this when she came back.

STEPHANIE. It was under the door.

CHLOE. Who's it from?

STEPHANIE. I think... Omar.

CHLOE reads. As she does so, STEPHANIE exits. Meanwhile, CHLOE's devastation grows with every line she reads.

CHLOE. Wuh... no...

MARK. What is it?

CHLOE. Take it. Get it away from me.

MARK. Chloe?

CHLOE. I, I can't. I can't breathe.

MARK. What's going on?

CHLOE. He broke up with me.

MARK. Who?

CHLOE. He just... no, no. This isn't... something's wrong. Something happened to him. He wouldn't just... I feel sick.

MARK. Was there anything today that might have hinted at –

CHLOE. No, no. I, well, I mean, he was a little weird, nervous, but then we talked and... I thought... we were going...

MARK. ...to the lecture?

CHLOE. What?

MARK. The lecture. Columbia. Is that –

CHLOE. Columbia? No. We were going to...

MARK. Is there, can I do anything for you?

CHLOE. *(mind racing)* Shhh.

MARK. It's okay. It's okay.

A long beat as CHLOE *pulls it together. Then:*

CHLOE. ...Well, congratulations. You must be really happy.

MARK. Is that what you think? I'm not like that, some monster.

CHLOE. But you knew this was going to happen.

MARK. I knew it could.

CHLOE. That it was likely.

MARK. I'm a paramedic, Chlo. I've been the only of us out there in the real world every day. And you don't... I never told any... I mean, I was there. Watching the bodies. Fall. Heard the collapse, like a, like a giant growling. Scraped the dust and ash and blood off my skin night after night, and after that. And after. And that's? Tip of the iceberg. My job, what I see, every day: pain, disease, murder, death. The things people do to each other, how they hurt each other. Can you blame me for calling you all here? I prayed for you, each of you, because I needed you to, to bring me some relief. Because this is what I know: one minute you can be walking through Battery Park and it's a beautiful day... next minute, it's... indescribable... I can't explain. I just want the beautiful day. I want that for me, I want that for you. After all, you were once my fake-wife. Still are.

CHLOE. ...We were gonna see America.

MARK. But America doesn't want to see you. Not like this.

CHLOE. No. I guess not.

MARK. Hey, I know what would lift your spirits. How about we go out, grab a bottle of wine, come back to the jacuzzi and drown our sorrows? Huh?

He helps her up, and as they head for the door:

CHLOE. You know what? I think I... you get the wine, I'll start the jacuzzi. Just wanna be alone for a bit. If that's okay.

MARK. *(goes to get his coat)* Yeah. Sure, sure.

CHLOE. Maybe some day, huh?

MARK. Some day what?

CHLOE. I don't know... I'll get to stand in front of the Grand Canyon at sunset, have some stranger take a picture of me and my husband?

MARK. ...Maybe.

He exits. CHLOE sits on the couch. A beat. She picks up the Dear John letter from the floor... and notices something on the nearby chair: OMAR's jacket. She crosses over to it. Holds it. Looks to the curtains, drawn for the very first time. She realizes. Sprints to the curtains, casts them aside. Sees OMAR. Throws the balcony door open. Drags OMAR inside. Is he dead? Sounds of wind as CHLOE climbs on top of OMAR, trying to warm him up. Sobbing.

CHLOE. No! No, baby. Please. Please, wake up. Come on. Here. That's warm, huh? Warmth. Can you feel that?

Please. Open your eyes. Open them, like you did for
me. It's your turn now. Open your eyes! Open them!

*CUE THE NEW, UPDATED THEME MUSIC. It's a
hipper version of the earlier one – signs of a show on
the outs. LIGHTS UP ON* [**LIVING ROOM – NEXT
SEASON**]. **MARK** *and* **FIONA** *are cutting up a fruit
salad.* **STEPHANIE** *'s on the couch, typing away on her
laptop. The acting feels heightened, desperate for laughs.*

FIONA. I love making fruit salad. It's so fun.

MARK. Isn't it?

FIONA. It's like throwing a block party. Hello, Mr. Strawberry.
Mind if I join you? Not at all, Mrs. Honeydew. ☺

MARK. And you, Mizz Papaya? How's your granddaughter?
Oh, she's a peach.

FIONA. *(taking* **MARK** *'s knife)* Okay, block party's over. ☺

CONNOR *bounds in from outside. He's happy as shit. He
stands behind* **STEPHANIE**, *who doesn't notice him. He
clears his throat. Once. Twice. Then, closes her laptop.*

STEPHANIE. Hey! This better be good. We're talking Brad-
Pitt-in-a-thong-good. ☺

CONNOR. Oh, it's Pitt-in-a-thong good, Mrs. Dash. Guess
who got a promotion AND a raise today?

STEPHANIE. You're kidding!

CONNOR. I love my job!

STEPHANIE. Wow! What's your new title?

CONNOR. Not sure.

STEPHANIE. The pay increase?

CONNOR. Not much.

STEPHANIE. Still expecting sex though?

CONNOR. Notwithstanding. *(they kiss)* ♥

BILLY. *(entering)* Did I hear sex? ☺

CONNOR. Just the word, Billy. Just the word. ☺

BILLY. How do I look? I got a date with Tina tonight.

MARK. Tina? I thought her name was Gina.

BILLY. No, that's who I dated last night. Or was it Lena?

STEPHANIE. I thought that was Nina.

CONNOR. Well, somebody's really got himself "ina" trouble. ☺

Entering the front door to huge audience APPLAUSE:
VERONICA.

VERONICA. Mail call!

MARK. Whatcha got there for us, Ronnie?

VERONICA. Bills, bills, bills. I've been living here since the fall, why do I keep getting Bill's mail? ☺

Everybody laughs. Nervously. Then sighs.

FIONA. Hey, that's weird.

STEPHANIE. What?

FIONA. This postcard. It's blank. All except for this one little word in the corner.

BILLY. What's it say?

The gang gathers around the postcard. But **MARK** *grabs it, rips it apart. BLACKOUT. LIGHTS UP on* **CHLOE** *standing alone, seemingly before a sunset. A beat, and* **OMAR** *enters. Puts his arms around her.*

CHLOE. Moscow.

The two smile. A camera lightbulb flashes.

END OF PLAY

PROPS:

$25,000 Pyramid
cardboard box, big enough for a small dog
DVD of *Patch Adams*
3 bags of crackers
a LaVyrle Spencer book
telescope
business card
cordless phone
letter in an envelope
garbage bag full of DVDs
Steinbeck's THE GRAPES OF WRATH
laptop
cheeze whiz & crackers
carton of milk
check in an envelope
ice cream containers
luggage
hammer
newspapers
coffee & mugs
big bag of clothing
gray wigs
phone headset
blanket
confirmation slip
duffel bag
2 Heineken
plastic GAP bag
pill bottle
wallet
pen & paper
fruit salad
postcard

Note: the most important prop here is the breast leaking device. In productions past, a simple tube with a liquid reservoir was taped to the actor's torso, and he was able to pump the liquid out by squeezing his arms. The pump was disguised by having the actor wear a T-shirt with a button-down shirt over it. Once the "leaking" started, the actor was able to show it off by opening the button-down for all to see.

SET

Should look like a typical set of a typical sitcom. Of note is that at the end of the first act, one of the wall flats must be able to fall down. In addition, the frame surrounding the front door must be able to – like a Buster Keaton stunt – collapse over Chloe. The fallen walls are then put back up during intermission, fully restoring the set for the top of act two.

COSTUMES

Most of the characters here are defined by their jobs: uniforms, or costumes associated with professions, are essential.

DORIS TO DARLENE
Jordan Harrison

Comedy / 4m, 2f / Unit Set

Doris to Darlene, A Cautionary Valentine: In the candy-colored 1960s, biracial schoolgirl Doris is molded into pop star Darlene by a whiz-kid record producer who culls a top-ten hit out of Richard Wagner's "Liebestod." Rewind to the candy-colored 1860s, where Wagner is writing the melody that will become Darlene's hit song. Fast-forward to the not-so-candy-colored present, where a teenager obsesses over Darlene's music -- and his music teacher. Three dissonant decades merge into an unlikely harmony in this time-jumping pop fairy tale about the dreams and disasters behind one transcendent song.

"Doris to Darlene: A Cautionary Valentine, at Playwrights Horizons, is a quirky and enjoyable love letter to music and its seductive power to make us lose ourselves… Harrison's language is by turns so punchy, poetic and observant."
- NY Daily News

"Mr. Harrison's play has an affectionate, music-loving heart."
- New York Times

"Doris to Darlene has much going for it: Harrison's intelligence, originality and passion."
- Time Out New York

"Harrison's teasing, rapturous chamber opera of a play spins and crackles like a beloved old 78 under a bamboo needle... Doris to Darlene is that rare thing: a rarefied theatrical experiment that has the glow of pure entertainment and the warmth of a folktale."
- Newsday

EURYDICE
Sarah Ruhl

Dramatic Comedy / 5m, 2f / Unit Set

In Eurydice, Sarah Ruhl reimagines the classic myth of Orpheus through the eyes of its heroine. Dying too young on her wedding day, Eurydice must journey to the underworld, where she reunites with her father and struggles to remember her lost love. With contemporary characters, ingenious plot twists, and breathtaking visual effects, the play is a fresh look at a timeless love story.

"RHAPSODICALLY BEAUTIFUL. A weird and wonderful new play - an inexpressibly moving theatrical fable about love, loss and the pleasures and pains of memory."
- The New York Times

"EXHILARATING!! A luminous retelling of the Orpheus myth, lush and limpid as a dream where both author and audience swim in the magical, sometimes menacing, and always thrilling flow of the unconscious."
- The New Yorker

"Exquisitely staged by Les Waters and an inventive design team… Ruhl's wild flights of imagination, some deeply affecting passages and beautiful imagery provide transporting pleasures. They conspire to create original, at times breathtaking, stage pictures."
- Variety

"Touching, inventive, invigoratingly compact and luminously liquid in its rhythms and design, Eurydice reframes the ancient myth of ill-fated love to focus not on the bereaved musician but on his dead bride -- and on her struggle with love beyond the grave as both wife and daughter."
- The San Francisco Chronicle

SAMUELFRENCH.COM

MAURITIUS
Theresa Rebeck

Comedy / 3m, 2f / Interior

Stamp collecting is far more risky than you think. After their mother's death, two estranged half-sisters discover a book of rare stamps that may include the crown jewel for collectors. One sister tries to collect on the windfall, while the other resists for sentimental reasons. In this gripping tale, a seemingly simple sale becomes dangerous when three seedy, high-stakes collectors enter the sisters' world, willing to do anything to claim the rare find as their own.

"(Theresa Rebeck's) belated Broadway bow, the only original play by a woman to have its debut on Broadway this fall."
- Robert Simonson, New York Times

"Mauritius caters efficiently to a hunger that Broadway hasn't been gratifying in recent years. That's the corkscrew-twist drama of suspense… she has strewn her script with a multitude of mysteries."
- Ben Brantley, New York Times

"Theresa Rebeck is a slick playwright… Her scenes have a crisp shape, her dialogue pops, her characters swagger through an array of showy emotion, and she knows how to give a plot a cunning twist."
- John Lahr, The New Yorker